Kill Crusade.

A black Harley r
It thundered up
the top. Every
rider crouching

The biker gunned ... ter aisle. He leaned into a ... skid at the front of the church and whipped the bike past the right front pews.

"What the hell?" Revere's voice boomed through the microphone. He stared at the man in the black visored helmet. He noticed the weapons crisscrossing the biker's chest now that he was still for a moment.

The man in black fired a machine-pistol burst four feet above the pews. "Everybody out!" The pistol waved them back.

The women screamed. The men shouted. In a panicked herd, they milled to the back of the church. They poured out of the rear exit like sand through an hourglass.

"What is it?" Revere shouted. "Are we under attack?"

The biker looked at Revere. He saw deacons reach for their guns and stare at the church doors. They expected an army to storm in.

"Answer me!" Revere shouted. "I said, are we under attack!"

"Damn right," the biker said. He pushed the black visored helmet over his head to show blond hair and a killing smile. Dartanian gunned the Harley past the deacons. The Skorpion M61 spit out a clip of 7.65mm stings. The first row of deacons crumpled.

Also by Rich Rainey:

THE PROTECTOR #1 VENUS UNDERGROUND

Rich Rainey

#2 THE PORN TAPES

PINNACLE BOOKS  NEW YORK

This is a work of fiction. All the characters and events portrayed in this book are fictional, and any resemblance to real people or incidents is purely coincidental.

THE PROTECTOR #2 THE PORN TAPES

An original Pinnacle Books edition, published for the first time anywhere.

First printing, June, 1983

ISBN: 0-523-41943-0

Cover illustration by George Wilson

Printed in the United States of America

PINNACLE BOOKS, INC.
1430 Broadway
New York, New York 10018

THE PORN TAPES

Prologue

The three drunks stopped shouting. They froze like attack dogs and listened to the footsteps on the dry summer pavement. Someone had the nerve to walk down Logan Avenue after midnight. It had to be a stranger.

T.L., Smith, and Cracker peered over the crumbling brick wall that separated their rat flat from the other houses. A man in rich threads walked towards them.

"The man's crazy," T.L. said.

Smith whistled under his breath. "Look at the fancy dude. Bet he's got enough loot to pay our lawyer's bill in one shot."

Cracker chose silence. He communicated best with his feet and fists. He liked to kick hell out of people, then crack their faces on the curb. That's why he hung with T.L. and Smith. They knew how to have fun.

"Wait!" T.L. hissed. "Let him pass. Then we take him."

The man was only six houses away on the dark street. House lights had blinked off one by one since the celebration began. The boys beat another rap. It was party time. The louder they screamed, the quicker came the darkness. No one wanted to see what the trio of thugs were up to. It was bad enough listening.

The man paused under the last bright lamppost. T.L. had smashed the rest with beer bottles and rocks. Beneath the quarter moon and lamp light, the man's features were clear. His blond hair was short. His deepset eyes scanned the rundown neighborhood. If he was lost he didn't appear too frightened. He looked like a man who'd seen worse places than this.

"That sucker's got some fight in him," T.L. crowed. "Been some time since we had what you'd call a challenge."

"Ain't never had a challenge," Smith said.

The scavengers lived off New Yorkers who thought muggers and killers always hit someone else. These three were indiscriminate. They'd hit anybody as long as the prey was alone. The gang was in for more than just money. They craved entertainment. Together they were real stomp artists.

Logan Avenue was their territory. Neighbors looked the other way when the tough boys strutted by in their tank tops. Their lean muscles and drug-fueled brains promised a wildness no one wanted to test.

Tonight's celebration was for the young couple they trashed in the park back in spring. The boy was in the hospital with boot marks on his face. They'd played football with him. He was the football. Smith and Cracker pinned him in a kneeling position with his head bent forward. T.L. performed the first kickoff. Two kickoffs and one crushed face later, they molested the girl.

The girl changed her testimony at the trial. T.L.'s lawyer had given him her address. He visited her and told her she was dead meat if she talked. "Put you in a coma just like your boyfriend," T.L. had threatened.

She listened hard. At the trial, she cried and said it was all a terrible mistake. Those three men had nothing to do with the assault.

Smart girl, T.L. thought. Not too smart, though. Some time soon, they'd knock on her door and throw her down for keeps. She was better dead.

The victory celebration was a class bash. They guzzled a case of beer and lit four sticks of dusted grass. After the bottles were smashed and smoke inhaled, they were restless for blood. Who should come along but this gift horse with a lot of bucks? Thanks to the blond dude, they could pay their lawyer man. He deserved every penny of his tab. After all, he showed them how to walk out of the courtroom as free men.

The man passed without looking down their alley. He walked to the chain-link fence and looked around. Beyond the fence was a condemned factory. Every window was shattered, every piece of salvageable equipment stolen. The cracked acre of tar that once served as a parking lot looked like the site of an earthquake.

"Ready for another kickoff?" T.L. asked.

Cracker laughed. He stepped out of the alley. T.L. and Smith followed. They debated if they should use knives, spiked knuckles, or beer bottles. "We could stone the sucker for a change," T.L. said.

They shuffled onto the street. It was going to be one hell of a night.

"It's a dead end, fuckhead," T.L. said.

Smith cackled. "Real dead."

The man looked at the three of them. He didn't

say a word. He stepped forward. That was odd, T.L. thought. Most cornered wimps backed up to the fence and waited for the first blow to come down. They were all sheep waiting for the mallet.

"Don't move, asshole," Smith said. "You stay right there."

The blond man advanced. There was no sign of fear on his face. That unsettled the three men who taunted him. What the hell was this? They got a guy cornered and he wasn't phased in the least. If they didn't outnumber him three to one, it might have been a scary situation.

"It's kickoff time," T.L. whooped. He sensed that any further delay would turn the tide against them. The guy *was* kind of scary, coming at them like that. "Hit 'im."

Cracker went first. The thick-shouldered goon ran full speed at the stranger and dove at his feet for a bone-smashing tackle.

The tackle didn't work. The blond man lifted his heel and jammed it into Cracker's face. There was a thud, a groan, and blood all over the street. T.L. stopped five feet away. So did Smith. What kind of shit was this? No one had ever stopped Cracker before.

The man worked swiftly while the two attackers hesitated. He twisted his foot slightly and poised it above Cracker's neck. He pushed down hard, stepping on Cracker as though he were a cockroach. The crunching sound was the worst part. This guy was an animal. Cracker was dead.

T.L. slotted his fingers into spiked brass knuckles and unsheathed the four-inch blade hidden in his leather belt. T.L. had seen it advertised in the survival magazines as a hidden defense against muggers. He bought his just in case he ran into one of those freaky bastards who carried it around. He stepped to the right of the blond man.

Smith moved to the left. "Lucky shot, motherfucker," Smith yelled. "But this time we ain't playing no game. This time we gonna kill you." He held a knife out in front of him, carving a wide circle. He danced and parried like a boxer shuffling in a ring, like he was an expert with a blade.

The blond man laughed. When the knife reached the apex of another sloppy circle, he kicked out in a blurring motion. A whooshing sound sang in the air as his left foot snapped into Smith's wrist. His arm shot over his head. The knife flew out of his hand. Smith screamed and spun around. Instinctively, he grabbed at his shattered wrist.

T.L. saw that the man had moved to cut them off. Now T.L. and Smith had the chain-link fence at their backs.

"Let us go," T.L. pleaded. "It was just a mistake, man, honest, we weren't going to hurt you. Just playing around." He clenched his left fist and cocked it back to his shoulder. If he had a chance, he was going to punch the spikes into the bastard's face. His right hand sweated on the copper hilt of the knife. "Be cool. We'll split. All right?"

The blond man reached inside his jacket. Smith saw the holster first and ran toward the fence. T.L. gasped. He felt a pain in his chest as the man pulled out a gleaming black machine pistol. The stock was folded over the barrel, curved with a stinger at the end. A ten-round clip curved from the bottom. A long tube was threaded on the end. It was silenced but ready to speak.

"Two hundred bucks, man," T.L. said. "It's all I got. I'll give it to you. All I got, all I got."

The man swung the machine pistol at him. "Skorpion M61," he said. "It's all I need."

T.L. ran. He headed for the other end of the street. He looked back, expecting to see the wicked pistol firing at him. But no, the man faced the other way.

He fired a Z pattern at Smith. Three rounds stung his ankles. Three more slanted up his hip. The last three chopped up his chest and hurled him into the chain-link fence. In the instant before he died, his eyes looked human for the first time. The look said that now he knew what his victims felt. The blood ran out of him quickly.

T.L. had almost reached safety. He looked back and saw Smith splattered for good. He saw Cracker stretched out. He saw the blond man walking toward him.

But T.L. was going to make it. There was the corner. Damn, if he could make it around the corner, he'd be free and clear. His sneakers skittered on the sidewalk as he sprinted for dear life. His breath gasped with each slamming stride. He was weak. Out of shape. He'd never been in a fight where someone hit back, a fight that lasted more than a couple of minutes. But he was going to make it. He was going to come back and kill that bastard.

He turned left onto an empty street. Good, he thought. One more block, another turn, down into the alley . . . *He'll never find me.*

An Oriental man stepped out of an alley. Japanese, Chinese. T.L. couldn't tell. Very thin. Very dark eyes. He wore loose pants and a black T-shirt. Oh shit, T.L. thought. He slowed down. This guy was just like the blond man. He had the same look. Even with the spiked knuckles and the knife,

T.L. knew he couldn't pass this man. Death greeted him in those eyes.

T.L. was good at kicking somebody in the head while Cracker and Smith held him. He was good at punching out anybody, as long as his buddies kept him still. But Cracker and Smith were dead. T.L. came to an awkward stop and turned around. He ran back past Logan Avenue and saw the man with the Skorpion walking his way.

He ran faster. He stumbled on the next curb and fell face first on the sidewalk. The scrapes on his cheek stung him with surprise. He didn't feel the pain, just the blood. Fear killed the raw and wet nerves. There would be no time to feel the pain later.

T.L. raced down the next block with a death grip on the knife. It was his last chance for survival. He wasn't going to let that go.

A third man stepped onto the sidewalk. He came from nowhere and blocked his way. He towered over T.L. *Sonofabitch, this was a setup*. These three men were making damned sure that no one walked out of Logan Avenue. The blond bastard had a backup squad to keep anyone from straying down the street while he did his work. No wonder he didn't seem too concerned about T.L. getting away. No wonder the Oriental didn't bother to chase him.

"NOOOO!" T.L. screamed. For the first time in his life, he charged another man one on one. He drew the knife back for a downward slash. With all his might, he slammed the blade home. An iron palm jackhammered into his wrist and squeezed. The knife fell. T.L. screamed in pain. He swung his spiked knuckles for the huge man's belly. Another palm grabbed that wrist and stopped it in mid-lunge. The man pushed both arms back. T.L. shouted as his arms snapped behind his back. The pain was white hot, like nothing he'd ever felt. It was taking him down to unconsciousness.

Before that could happen, the man took out an Ingram M10 and kicked him into hell with ten whispering 9mm Parabellum slugs. The two other men walked swiftly and silently to him, as he holstered the Ingram inside his black windbreaker.

"Court's adjourned," the blond man said.

At the next block, the three men climbed into a beat-up white Chevy that looked like it fit in with the neighborhood. The blond man drove the cutaway car a quarter mile before abandoning it for their real set of wheels. They hopped into a silver Audi 5000 and roared off into the dark, breezy night.

The bodies would be discovered at dawn. The media would squawk about the brutal slaying of three bright young men. When the rap sheets came out, the media would do an about-face and say it was high time that street thugs got what they deserved. Something good was happening in America.

What was happening was the Protector.

Alex Dartanian was first tagged the Protector in 1974. That was the year the CIA purged 1200 covert specialists from the ranks. That was the year Dartanian Security Service was established. Dartanian's blond hair and computer-calm eyes often flashed on New York newscasts. Television cameras zoomed in on the celebrities under his guard and then were drawn irresistibly to him. There was a quality about Dartanian that the cameras loved. He carried himself with an aura of total control that outshined the most glamorous New York starlet. His blue eyes invited trust or panic. They were windows into a gentle, complex man. Or they were the icy gaze of an assassin. People obeyed those eyes, because there was six feet of iron behind it. The nicely cut pinstriped suits could not hide the lithe body within, always ready to strike.

The TV people needed a label for the striking blond man. They called him the Protector after he prevented the assassination of a corporate executive testifying against a board of directors looting the company coffers. Dartanian wasted the hit team that came at him in broad daylight. It was all legal and above board. It established his credentials. Dartanian's protection was lethal and final. He didn't back down.

The bodyguard assignments were good for business and established a cover for Dartanian, but they were just a fraction of his interests. Dartanian Security Service cut a byzantine path through every level of society. DSS was an international operation, a smooth, overt security machine.

But there was a ghost in the machine. It's name was ICE. Inner Court Executions. That was the strongest arm of DSS. Covert, deadly, and just, ICE was the ultimate court. Alex Dartanian was the ultimate jury.

Hundreds of operatives worked for DSS. Less than 40 knew that ICE existed. They had to prove themselves in DSS before being recruited to the heart of the operation. ICE was the heart. Dartanian was the soul.

Dartanian had enough pull to have stayed with the CIA if he'd wanted, but it was time to go out on his own. There were too many messiahs in the intelligence cult, too many factions. From month to month, the infighting changed the direction of the agency. Rather than work for superiors who caved in to outside pressure, Dartanian chose to work for himself.

The public reason for the forced retirement of so many expert agents in 1974 was a desire to harness a CIA out of control. The agency spokesmen said it was time to halt the covert activities before the whole world became a Watergate. The real reason was a split over détente within the agency. Most of the purged agents were hardline anti-Soviets who considered détente a sham. Even while Russia proclaimed a desire for closer relations with the U.S., they supplied the terrorist network with funds, weapons, training camps, and cover operations. It didn't matter what the cause was. Any group that brought chaos and terror to the Western world was eligible.

Like so many other agents, Dartanian knew that the Russian bear never changed colors. He still maintained close ties with the CIA, but his security work for them was on a selective basis. Dartanian chose his own operations. If they coincided with the agency, good. If not, there was no one to say no to him.

Right after the first CIA purge, invisible empires sprang up across America. Ex-operatives offered their skills to the private sector. Oil companies set up their own armies of former agents. Politicians hired dirty-tricks specialists to wreck their opponents. Computer cartels hired "hacks" who could penetrate competing corporate data banks and loot million-dollar secrets. Left and right extremists hired the weapons experts. The spooks haunted America. Those who sold their services to the highest bidder were known as "blackhats." Those who only helped companies in the American interest were "whitehats."

Since it was good for business to appear connected to the intelligence agencies, most of the security outfits created a mystique about themselves. It was their nature to throw up a cloak around their activities. Some companies *were* fronts for the CIA. They were staffed by "purged" agents who worked for the agency and no one else. Others were outright mercenary outfits that sold CIA secrets to anyone with the right price.

A shadowy network spanned the country. Right in the middle of them was DSS. The Cage Street headquarters in midtown Manhattan was a complete intelligence agency unto itself. Dartanian's command center was on the penthouse floor of the ten-story, marble-and-mirrored-glass structure.

From his large office suite, Dartanian planned his ICE operations. He had a computer system linked with NADDIS, EPIC, and a dozen more intelligence banks. The lower five floors of the DSS building were taken by the CIA, NSA, DEA, Interpol liaisons, and tactical police squads. It was a cop shop, spook exchange, and all-around law enforcement cabal. Operatives shuffled back and forth from the government agencies to DSS, exchanging fronts, intelligence, and physical support. The top five floors were all controlled by DSS. There was an armament company, a computer service, a half-dozen front corporations, and the above-ground DSS operations.

Behind all of that, the reason for its existence, was ICE. As DSS became an established entity on the local scene, Alex cut down the number of personal bodyguard assignments. He handled some celebrities when they requested him and no one else—if the case fit in with his purposes. Dartanian infiltrated every level of society on the assignments. He looked into the hearts of corporate giants when he established security systems for them. He followed the web of connections between celebrities and the media machines that controlled the perceptions of the American public.

When the Eighties arrived, Dartanian's invisible arm reached the peak of its powers. It was time to bring that arm down. It was time to bring on the new ICE age.

Mick Porter and Sin Simara had been ICE agents from the beginning. Dartanian had worked with Porter in Vietnam during Operation Phoenix. He hooked up with Simara in the New China theater where Simara was CIA liaison with Taiwan intelligence. Dartanian had walked through the fire with both men. They were hard to forget. When he left the agency, they were his first recruits.

Sin Simara was the product of a Japanese warlord and a Chinese wife from Shanghai. His father combined a black-market past with a military-intelligence future during the Second World War years. Sin Simara grew up in a Samurai household. As a child, he was exposed to a dozen martial arts and secret societies of postwar Japan that revolved around his father. Simara was a natural for CIA recruitment when he came of age. His warrior code made him even more of a natural for ICE.

Mick Porter cut off a promising pro-football career for another type of draft. He enlisted in the army and was selected for Special Forces training. That led him to the jungles of Vietnam. After living in the north in enemy territory for a year,

Mick's four-man SF team was nailed in a Cong crossfire that left three dead and one near dead. Mick wandered in the jungle, half dead, with a bounty on his head while the Cong hunted him.

Mick had expected to die a million miles away from home. Then a CIA commando in blackface popped out of the jungle and asked him if he wanted to go south for the winter. The man's name was Alex Dartanian, and Mick swore that he would stand up with him anywhere in the world.

He got the chance to stand with Dartanian in ICE. Mick and Sin Simara accompanied the blond headman from the beginning. They formed a triad that was nearly invincible as it ran through the jungles of American cities.

The Logan Avenue icing was a typical ICE operation. The ICE computers locked onto the three repeat creeps who continually littered the police blotter. Murder, mugging, and rape were their specialties. Dartanian studied their rap sheets and cased their neighborhood hideout. He sent a man to investigate the molested girl's story. She was afraid to speak because of death threats, but the ICE agent got the story from the friends and family she had confided in. Posing as a cop, the ICE agent collected information on all of the trio's victims. It was always the same story. No matter how many murders were traced to the three men, none of the witnesses ever talked. They were always reached with death threats just before the trial.

It wasn't that they knew how to beat the system. The system beat itself. Punishment was a thing of the past. Even if the trashmen got convicted for murder, they were still out in ten years for good behavior.

It was time for a new system.

One

Melonie Grand drifted down the sixth-floor hallway of the Colony Hotel on the arms of Curt Bonner, one of nine leading men in her latest porn film. She was blond, wore a snug white sweater and clinging gray skirt, and faked the breathless raspy voice of Marilyn Monroe whenever she met the public.

Starlet was Melonie's big chance for a major score. The publicity for the flick based on the seamier aspects of Marilyn Monroe's career hailed it as the *Deep Throat* of the Eighties. *Starlet* was the first big-budget crossover flick. *Starlet* would smash all box-office records. *Starlet* was Melonie Grand's tenth hard-core film.

Hype for the unfinished picture was confusing at first. Promo ads in the sex trades cast Melonie as the next Linda Lovelace. They also portrayed her as the new Marilyn Monroe. This left the public with an image of a schizophrenic sex star. Who was she really?

When the stills from the picture were released to the magazines, she was promoted as the new Marilyn. The powers behind the film decided to go for the classy screen-siren image. From that point on,

Melonie Grand became Marilyn Monroe. Spiked heels, fishnet stockings, tight skirts and clinging sweaters were her basic uniform.

Melonie courted the media three or four nights a week. Now that shooting was almost complete, Melonie had more time to hype *Starlet*. The agenda was inhuman. She was always "on." But according to the hype, Melonie Grand was inhumanly beautiful, a goddess who surpassed Marilyn's well-known figure, and goddesses needed no rest.

Tonight would be a replay of the last two nights. Down in the hotel bar, a group of out-of-town reporters waited for their interviews. Half of them would be drunk and on the make. The other half would just be drunk.

After the interviews with this group of reporters, Melonie had a late dinner date with an influential film columnist. She couldn't remember his name or the magazine. It didn't matter. Melonie's manager said the man had clout. She would keep the date.

Ah well, she thought, what else could a poor rich girl do but get on with it? She tightened her grip on Curt's arm, sighed, and walked down the hall.

A white-haired man fumbled with his room key and did a double-take when he saw Melonie. "My God!" he said. "You look just like—"

"Thank you," Melonie said. "I know." She smiled and stared at his eyes. The man was in shock. A time machine had just dropped Marilyn Monroe in his lap. He looked at her stiletto heels, her full sweater, and her wavy yellow hair. He turned his head and watched her until she cut around the corner.

Melonie had no misgivings about the effect she had on him. It was all product. All illusion. She was climbing on the back of Marilyn Monroe's image. Just as Marilyn chose her path to climb to the top, Melonie followed in the same high-heeled footsteps. She was a walking pinup, a glossy doll come to life.

Curt Bonner shot for the Clark Gable look and missed. He looked like an ordinary man trying to dress up as Gable on Halloween. It wasn't Curt's looks that made him a leading man.

Melonie enjoyed being with him the most. He was genuinely nice. No macho crap with Curt. He had nothing to prove. He looked on the porn business as a way of making a living. He fell into it ten years ago and never climbed out. It beat hell out of zapping hogs in the slaughterhouse where he used to work.

"Ready for the twenty questions?" Melonie asked.

"I'll be lucky to get one. Nobody notices me when I'm with you."

"Ohhhh," she purred. "Poor baby." Melonie caressed his smooth cheek and pouted sympathy in her best Marilyn Monroe fashion. She noticed a look in his eyes that said he wished for a moment he was Clark Gable and she was Marilyn Monroe going out for a night on the town.

The elevator was in the middle of the next corridor. Just as they reached it, a man popped around the far corner. He wore a shiny maroon suit too tight for his stocky frame. It was a relic from ten years ago, the last time it had been pressed.

He didn't belong in the Colony Hotel. The trendy hotel catered to middle-range celebrities who had just about arrived or were on their way down. Most of the residents had some sort of connection with the arts business. It was a fashionable pickup place with four bars and a ballroom. It swung. This man didn't.

His gray hair was curly and short. His tie was knotted too thick. Melonie shuddered when he looked at her. It wasn't due to a lustful gaze. She was immune to that. What disturbed her was the emptiness in those eyes. He looked at her body and her face, but it was almost like he was trying to identify her. Weird.

He passed them.

"What's wrong?" Curt said. "You feel cold all of a sudden."

"Nothing," she lied. She looked over her shoulder. The man stopped at the end of the hall. He reached inside his jacket and turned around. His hand came out full of metal. A long-barreled revolver seemed to grow in his hand. *Oh God, oh my God,* she thought. It was so unreal. Why? It aimed for her face.

"*Gun*!" she screamed. "He's got a—"

Curt turned around and instinctively stepped in front of her. Two blasts jerked his head back and lifted his feet off the floor. He tumbled into the closed elevator well and streaked the doors with gushing blood.

Melonie tripped over her feet in her rush to get away. A third blast from the gun knocked a fist-size hole in the wall at the end of the corridor. It would have taken off the back of her head if she hadn't fallen.

She scrambled and crawled and willed her way down to the end of the hall. *Stupid clinging skirt, goddamn high heels*. Her palm smacked against the smooth gray door around the corner. She pushed it open and jump-skipped down to the next landing. Her high heels clattered behind her. One of the straps stuck to her after she kicked them off. Melonie screamed and swore and made it to the next landing when a slug cracked into the steps in front of her.

She looked up and saw him lining up on her again like it was a duck shoot. The echo from the blast shot down her screams. Melonie dove down six more steps to avoid the next blast. She didn't stop running after that. His rapid footsteps and the heavy thump of his jumps to the landings kicked her past her breaking point. She hurried her fear-iced body down another landing and then jerked open the door to the second floor. Melonie ran out into the hall screaming for her life.

A middle-aged man poked his head out the door to see what the commotion was about. Melonie kicked the half open door and barreled into his room. She slammed the door behind her and locked it.

The man stared at her. He was a strait-laced businessman type who probably yanked open the door to yell about the noise. Now he didn't know what to make of her.

Melonie caught her breath. She thought about the man who tried to kill her. He looked so normal. Just a guy in a square suit. About forty. She'd seen thousands like him. Except for the eyes, she thought. She'd never forget those chilling blank eyes.

"He tried to kill me!" she said. "Me. I'm Melonie fucking Grand, and he tries to kill me. Will you look at me? Will you look at this getup I'm in? Who in their right mind would try to kill Marilyn Monroe!"

It was a first for Melonie. Men had tried just about everything with her. But no one had ever shot at her before.

* * *

"Another bottle?" Robert Edge asked. His face was red with a boozy glow. It was habit with him. After every day's shooting on *Starlet*, he took his live-in mate and fellow porn star, Mona Leese, to the Canterbury Restaurant on Park Avenue. They both had the good looks of soap-opera stars, although their careers were light years away. People recognized them but didn't know how.

Mona Leese nodded. She brushed her straight, dark-red hair out of her eyes. She affected a witchy look. A mysterious exotic creature at large. She was so above it all, so bored with the wild attention she attracted from such a mundane thing like porn.

The waiter replaced the empty bottle of claret. Robert and Mona relaxed in the thick, cushioned leather chairs and chatted across their favorite table. It was time to get lit.

"I think the gentlemen recognizes you," Robert said.

Mona sipped her wine and looked at the man in the dark suit standing a half-dozen tables away. He looked like he wouldn't ever be caught dead in a porn theater, but you never could tell. Maybe he was one of the autograph hounds. She did have a dedicated following. Men loved to say they met Mona Leese in person.

"Here he comes. Give him a thrill?"

"Why not?" Mona said. She leaned forward as the man approached with a pen and spiral notebook in hand. Her cleavage spilled out of the black V-shaped bodice. It was enough to make a man weak in the knees.

"Are you Mona Leese?" the man asked.

She looked from his eyes down to her cleavage. "Can't you tell?"

He laughed and looked away from her show of flesh. He dropped the small notebook in front of her. "Can I have your autograph?"

"Sure. Who shall I make it out to?"

"The devil," he said. He took out a small automatic from his side pocket and shot Mona Leese in the head. She jerked back into the chair. He spun and shot Robert Edge in the chest and the stomach. He turned back to Mona and shot her one more time as her head slumped onto the table.

At the sound of the first shot, everybody in the restaurant dived under their tables. Dignified waiters dropped to the floor and crawled. Women screamed into the plush carpet, and men prayed they wouldn't get it.

The man picked up the notebook and trotted out of the restaurant.

The cream-colored Cadillac Seville coasted to a stop in the parking loop in front of Le Black Cat. An attendant with a silver cap and silver epaulets opened the doors for *Starlet* lead man Ben Chaser and three small-time porn actresses. The women danced onto the sidewalk like royalty and headed toward the nightclub entrance.

"The wheels are new," Ben said. "Take it easy, huh, pal?" He slipped the attendant a five. Before he let go of the bill, he said, "Not too fast. Right?"

The silver cap nodded and climbed into the Caddy. When Ben Chaser caught up to the women, the attendant strafed the four of them with a full clip from a Walter MPL submachine gun. The 9mm slugs mowed them down like bowling pins.

He drove the Caddy away. Slow.

Two

Alex Dartanian tossed two folders onto his desk. They skimmed over the black surface and struck the desk-top computer. Several 8" x 10" photos spilled from the top folder. Half were surveillance shots of Melonie Grand. The others were reductions of the Melonie posters that were flooding the market. They ranged from hardly clothed to fully naked.

The ICE computer had printed a lot of data on the yellow-haired siren and her manager. Pornography figures were heavily investigated by government agencies for possible connections to the drug trade and cash-laundering schemes. The DEA, FBI, IRS, and local police units funneled input to NADDIS and EPIC, which in turn served as data pools for select intelligence agencies—and ICE. The electronic rap sheets were exhaustive.

Melonie Grand was a walking wet dream for millions of fans. Someone had tried to slaughter her. She had an appointment with Dartanian in ten minutes.

Dartanian lit a Pall Mall. He sat on the window ledge that looked down on Cage Street from the DSS building. It was an oasis of calm bordered by corporate and residential towers stacked next to each other like a row of monstrous dominoes. A wave of fear and crime had almost toppled those dominoes. But it was his city now. The dominoes would not fall.

Except for the hand that lifted the cigarette, Alex was as still as the gargoyles standing sentry over the tall gray buildings around him. He was thinking about Melonie Grand. He was thinking about ICE. It was a 24-hour obsession. It had to be. There were a lot of years and an army of modern vampires between his dream and the reality.

He stubbed out the filterless butt and grabbed the second folder. It contained the seedy life of Drew Wilson, a hustler for 20 of his 35 years, who considered himself another Dale Carnegie in the making. He worked phony land sales, sold encyclopedias that never made it to the buyer's house, and ran a score of mail-order rackets. Any time one of his mail-order operations received an injunction, he shut it down and started another one. If people were foolish enough to send him money through the mail, that was their problem.

Wilson graduated to securities frauds and rubber-check passing before he ended up in Dannemora Prison. When he came out, porn was the quickest way to make a buck. He sold a college girl named Melonie a dream of instant stardom. She was still paying for it ten years later.

"Miss Grand and her manager to see you." Diane Cummings, the day receptionist, buzzed him from the outer suite.

"Send them in."

If Marilyn Monroe had walked into his office,

the effect would be the same. Melonie continued the famous persona, despite the attempt on her life. In fact, she improved upon it. Melonie was gifted with a better body. There was more to her than Marilyn ever had. Every inch of it was nicely packed in a Fifties-style sweater-and-slacks set. She nodded at Dartanian and dropped into one of the soft brown leather chairs that ringed his desk.

Drew Wilson looked closer to 50 than 40. He was gaunt and ax-faced. The back of his head was thick and round, but the front tapered to a hawk nose beneath a slanting forehead. His cheeks were tucked in like he was smoking a pipe. A pursuit of decadence had worn off any excess flesh from the man. He favored a tweedy-professor look that was all wrong. He belonged in sharkskin.

After the introductions, Dartanian let him talk for a while to get a fix on him. Wilson loved to be in charge. He chattered endlessly in a salesman's rap, expecting Dartanian to nod in agreement at his ideas.

"So we'll spring for around-the-clock protection," Drew said. "I'll go over it with you how I want it, and then you can explain it to your men. Got it?"

"Have you ever done security work before?" asked Dartanian.

"No, but I got a lotta good ideas. Hey, come on, I'm as sly as the next guy. Security is security, man. We just have to blanket the babe here until the flick's wrapped." He tapped his gem-harnessed fingers on the leather arm. He looked around at the expensively furnished office. "Hey, looks like you're doing all right. How do you get into this security gig?"

"Pretend you're not a cheap hustler for the next half hour and you can stay," Dartanian said. "If not, I'll toss your ass out of here."

"Hey, you can't insult Drew Wilson like that!"

"It's easier than you think. Now sit down or take a walk."

Wilson slumped into his chair. Melonie hid a smile beneath her blood-red fingernails.

Dartanian went over the ground rules. His decision was final on all security matters. They had to give every bit of information he asked for, no matter how powerful the name or organization, and they had to be clean. If he discovered any connections between them and dirty money, he would drop them.

"You're some kind of guy," Wilson said. "Shit, man, it's dangerous to talk about people in this business."

"It's dangerous not to. I have to know everything I'm dealing with to put a stop to the hits."

Wilson nodded. "Dig this, man. The money's clean. Buncha boy scouts are backing this deal."

"Good. Then there's nothing to worry about." Dartanian looked at Melonie. She hadn't said a word yet. She was so used to letting Wilson speak for her that she automatically took a back seat. "Miss Grand, if you would describe what happened at the hotel, we'll start from there."

"She was doing pub for—"

Dartanian cut him off with a wave of his hand. "Melonie?"

The ghost of Marilyn Monroe talked to him in a husky rasp. She described the man who came for her, the way Curt Bonner died, her flight, and what she believed was a second attempt on her life at her upper west side flat.

Her knowledge of the other hits was just what she read in the newspapers. She was in a state of shock but wasn't totally incapacitated by the trauma. She felt like an actress in a movie. It was too crazy to be real.

Melonie Grand couldn't think of one reason why anyone wanted her dead.

"I can think of several," Dartanian said. "Maybe you're caught in the middle of someone else's war. Maybe Drew has a lot of enemies. Maybe the backers are mixed up in something that started all this. There's another maybe and that's the worst one. Maybe it's just some lunatic calling the shots."

"He looked so strange. I'll never forget the way he looked at me. It wasn't natural." Melonie stroked fluffy bangs out of her eyes. She looked at Dartanian as a child would a father. For once she wasn't solely in the hands of a hustler like Drew Wilson.

"What's important is that we finish the movie," Drew said. "I got everything riding on this deal. It took a long time to get here."

"Is that your only interest?" Dartanian said.

"Hey, naturally, I want to protect Melonie. Let's face it, friend, I'm the one who made her what she is today."

Dartanian shook his head. His eyes made it plain that he'd seen a thousand Drew Wilsons before. They bred like flies. He leaned forward over his desk to speak with Melonie. "I hate to say this, but I agree with Wilson. It's best that we finish the movie. Of course, I have a different reason."

"I'm open to suggestions," Melonie said.

"I guess you are," Drew snickered.

"Interrupt me again," Dartanian said, "and you go out the window instead of the door."

Drew was about to speak but thought better of it. Dartanian could tell the man thought he was holding back a trump card. Let him think what he wants.

"I can provide security, Melonie. I can teach you security methods. But six months from now, they can take you off the map in the time it takes to pull a trigger. We have to assume that they're gunning for you no matter how long it takes. The best way to stop them is to control the circumstances of the hit. You make some appearances. You finish shooting the movie. But let me arrange it. When they try for the hit, we put them down."

Melonie nodded. "You want me to be bait."

"Sometimes."

"I like it," Drew said.

"It's up to you," Dartanian said to Melonie. "I'll provide security that will keep you under lock and key, or I'll set a trap for the creeps. You decide this point. After that, I make all the decisions."

"We'll do it your way," Melonie said. She was nervous. She worried her lower lip with her pearly whites and shrank slightly into the soft leather chair like it was a cocoon.

"Good. From this point on, you're under my protection. You stay where I want you to stay, and move when I say move."

"Where you gonna keep her?" Drew asked.

"I'll let you know if the need comes up."

"What! Who do you think you're dealing with?" Drew Wilson shot up from the chair. "Come on, sweet stuff, we're booking out of here." He snapped his finger and motioned for Melonie to get up. He turned to Dartanian and threw down his trump card. "Look, pal, I only came to you because the backers said to pay you a visit and check you out. But that's it. I did my duty and now we're going elsewhere." He turned and saw that Melonie hadn't moved. "Get your ass in gear."

"I want him," Melonie said.

"Look, who's in charge here?"

"He is," Melonie said.

Drew sputtered and looked foolish, but he wasn't about to walk out on his meal ticket. He wanted to kick something. He wanted to scream. He buried his hands in his pockets and muttered about unfaithful women.

"Sit down," Dartanian said. "We've got a lot of talking to do."

The first debriefing of Melonie Grand and Drew Wilson took two hours. In that time, Dartanian got a star's-eye view of the porn world. Melonie's information checked out with her dossier, although she glossed over the years she spent doing porn loops. She spoke about her art and considered herself a true actress. They all did, Dartanian thought. It justified the weird performances demanded from them.

Dartanian discussed her well-publicized memoir-in-the-making. Wilson called it a 'fuck and tell' book. Formerly the province of has-been actresses, the new scandal books focused on hot numbers in their prime. Fanne Foxe, Liz Ray, and Linda Lovelace paved the way. It was Melonie's turn to bare her all.

"That's reason enough for a paranoid fat cat to gun for you. If you name names, you might ruin careers. That's the major attraction, right? To see the high and mighty fall?"

Melonie shrugged off Dartanian's question. "The book's not even written yet," she said. "I'm taping myself at the moment to dredge up the memories. The trick is to name names without mentioning specific individuals. That's the selling point. What famous TV star's a pervert? Who's banging whom in Hollywood?"

"We keep it a guessing game," Wilson said. "For legal reasons."

"I want all your tapes," Dartanian said. "And I want you to make a list of everybody you've knocked into since you started in the business. Don't hold back."

Melonie nodded. "Anything you say," she cooed.

Another area he probed was the backing for *Starlet*. The money for the flick came from Taplin Corporation, a computer-software outfit expanding into the videotape market. Dartanian's fingers whisked over the soft-touch keyboard on the desk-top computer as he talked. A Dun and Bradstreet financial analysis of the company appeared on the CRD screen. The Taplin Corporation was a billion-dollar monster with a half-dozen communications subsidiaries. That explained the extravagant publicity for *Starlet* to complement the big budget. Press junkets, posters, magazine promos, billboards, and a gala premier were all being bankrolled by the company. *Starlet* was destined to break all box-office records for a porn film, and perhaps even for a mainstream film.

The subject was tantalizing. *Starlet* focused on Marilyn Monroe's bed-hop to the top as a producer's plaything. Also featured were Monroe's rumored stag films and her alleged affairs with the Kennedy brothers. Her numerous escapades accounted for the nine leading men starring opposite Melonie Grand. Three of those men were dead. Four bit-part actresses also got caught in the most extreme form of censorship ever to hit the porn world.

The more Dartanian talked with Melonie, the more suspects turned up. Perhaps someone in the

Taplin organization was dead set against getting mixed up in porn. Maybe it was someone who had a good chance of landing in Melonie's memoir. It could be anybody.

It was ironic to see Melonie Grand sitting across from Dartanian's desk. She had weathered ten years of life in the porn chain, moving up from the loops to full-length features. Now she was at the top. Her old movies were being collected for reissue on videotape. Her new movie was destined to smash the crumbling wall between mainstream flicks and porn—if she lived to complete it. Melonie was number one on an assassin's hit parade.

She was positive another attempt had been in the making. After she gave her statement to the police, Melonie went back to her place and spent the night looking out her window for boogeymen. They came after midnight. Two men stood across the street and studied her darkened bedroom window. One looked like the bastard that wasted Curt Bonner. She didn't stick around to find out. Melonie skipped out the back entrance of the three-story brownstone and ran two blocks. She caught a Columbus Avenue cab working the late-night restaurants and took it to Drew Wilson's place.

He was coking it up with an actress trying to break into porn. Drew couldn't protect her against anything tougher than a summer breeze, but at least it was a place to stay. At least she wasn't alone.

Dartanian let Melonie talk, questioning her only when she strayed off course. It was no problem to get Drew rapping away. He gloried in his clever manuevering that brought Melonie to the big time. Dartanian learned that Drew was wonderful. He was also brilliant. Good to kids. Generous to the rookie actresses on the way up. Finally, Dartanian had to cut him off just as he was about to take credit for the gentle summer day sweeping through Manhattan.

"I've got another appointment coming up," Dartanian said. "Drew, I want you to get me Melonie's agenda for the next month. I also want you to be available. My agents Sin Simara and Mick Porter will be handling you. Cooperate with them as you would with me."

"Sure. What about Melonie?"

"She'll be in a safe place," Dartanian said. "I'd recommend that you move out of your apartment until this blows over. Coordinate your safeguards with Sin Simara."

"I don't need a babysitter," Drew said. "This boy can take care of himself."

"It's up to you. I'm providing security for Melonie. I can provide it for you, if you want."

Drew leaned over Melanie's chair and caressed her under the chin. "Look, kid, this'll be over in a couple of days, and we can get on with making you the best thing since Mom's apple pie."

Melonie gave him a "get lost" smile. When he left, she turned on the real thing. "It's just the two of us now," she said. "What have you got in mind?"

"First, drop that breathless bit. Second, if you will wait outside for a half hour, I can take care of some business and then take care of you."

"Oh, Alex," she said, breathless as ever. "Just tell me what to do and I'll do it." She took his hand, stood up, and then bounced out of his office like she was on her way to a tryst with JFK.

Dartanian kicked his heels onto the desk. He tilted the plush black swivel chair as far back as it could go, and visualized the path in front of him. Porn straddled the underground and straight worlds. It was secretive and suspect. It wasn't going to welcome him with open arms.

He stretched forward to push the dossiers of Melonie and Drew aside. A soft hum sounded when he ejected the microcassette from the hidden desktop recorder. He labeled the cassette. The operation had begun.

For the next half hour, Dartanian took care of DSS affairs. In the last minutes, he admitted Walt Garrick into his office. Garrick was a DEA operative who ran a squad of undercovers from the third floor of the Cage Street building.

The DEA borrowed Sin Simara to pose as a buyer for an incoming freighter of heroin packed inside chocolate-dust crates from Stockholm. Simara had spent so much time infiltrating tribal drug lords in Thailand, Burma, and Nam that he had no trouble sliding into the New York drug scene. When he turned on the evil, no one took him for heat.

The DEA requested Simara frequently. Dartanian lent him whenever possible. He owed the DEA, just as the DEA owed Dartanian. The armed yacht and cigarette boat used in the recent ICE operation against the Venus Underground white slavers came from the DEA.

"See if you can clinch the white sale tomorrow at the latest," Dartanian said. "I'm running on empty without Simara."

"Tell you what," Garrick said. "I'll contact the dope kingpin and tell him we've got other busts to make. And we'd really appreciate if he could deliver a day early. How's that?"

Dartanian shrugged. "If that's the best you can do. . . ." He laughed when Garrick rolled his eyes heavenward. "Keep me posted on the bust. I need my man as soon as possible."

"You got it," Garrick said, and left the room.

He was replaced by a much-easier-on-the-eye Melonie Grand. She couched herself in the leather chair facing Dartanian. She flashed him a pair of "gee whiz" eyes. With a breathless rasp, she said, "You know, I did an awful lot of thinking while I was waiting."

Dartanian wondered if she could ever drop the siren act. Murder didn't seem to put a dent in her see-through armor. "Did you happen to think of a reason why someone is trying to kill you?"

Melonie responded with a dreamy stare. "Ever since I started in this business, Alex, I thought I'd be punished someday for what I was doing. But never like this."

Three

Mick Porter lived through Nam. He survived ICE wars across the globe. He'd done just about everything a paladin could do, except guard the fetching body of a porn actress while she did her stuff.

Melonie Grand stood fifteen feet away from the former Special Forces man. Incandescent klieg lights pinned her to the lush set that duplicated Marilyn Monroe's Fifties-style bedroom. She was half turned toward Mick, with one hand resting on her luscious hip. Tan stockings with white lace borders climbed her thighs. White garter straps led the way to a half-inch-thick garter belt above the bare cheeks of her ass. A wine-colored camisole pushed up her breasts, rounded them, and presented them as a top-shelf treat to the eyes.

A sandy-haired actor who vaguely resembled Jack Kennedy stood beside Melonie. Both listened to the man in black chinos and white shirt as he choreographed the coming scene. Peter Cruz was the writer-director for *Starlet*. As an independent creator of television commercials, he won three Clio awards. When he moved into porn, he won the Erotic Academy Award for Best Film with his first feature. Cruz went on to make four of the biggest box-office porn films of the Seventies. He knew how to advertise a product whether it was a bag of corn chips or a 38-25-36 Melonie Grand.

Mick sighed. It was his job to keep a close eye on the client. That could be painful at times. There were two more barely dressed actresses on the set who seemed to enjoy teasing him. Two cameramen with Paniflex equipment and a stunning redhead named Barbara completed the crew. Barbara handled the lights, makeup, and "special effects." Even though she was dressed in cheeky cutoffs and a purple midriff, Mick enjoyed looking at her more than the practically naked actresses.

Mick was drowning in a sea of flesh in the Fairfax. The West 49th Street hotel had been dubbed Silicon Valley by the DSS agents who guarded the overly buxom starlets. The hotel was owned by the Taplin Corporation and had been used for a major part of the filming. That also made the security arrangements easier. Since the backers owned the hotel, Dartanian was able to work out a defense for Melonie with a free hand.

That defense called for Mick Porter to be on hand every day. He alternated assignments with street agents in parked cars. A radio man directed them from the fifth floor of the hotel.

Mick preferred working the street. It wasn't so claustrophobic. Up here with the sweet treats, he was definitely overdressed. Beneath his light beige suit, he carried an Ingram M10 room sweeper in a shoulder holster. On his right hip sat a Heckler & Koch P7 self-cocking automatic pistol. Both used 9mm magazines. With the eight-shot pistol and the Ingram submachine gun, he was ready for a firefight. For added insurance, he wore a lightweight Matthews Police bulletproof vest under his shirt.

Dartanian was similarly loaded for bear. Along with his Skorpion M61 machine pistol, he carried a concealed ASP 9mm pistol. Neither showed under his weapon-tailored, blue pin-stripe suit. He spent most of his time talking to Peter Cruz, studying Melonie's agenda, or sweeping the street below with a Bushnell 7x50 binocular. The radio man in the next suite used a higher magnification binocular on a tripod and instantly reported any unusual traffic patterns. But Dartanian liked to get the feel of the street himself.

Mick studied Alex for a moment, impressed by his calm. Alex didn't see a room full of jiggling flesh. He saw a client and nothing more. Mick saw a brace of nymphs running around like monkeys in a 35mm cage.

Peter Cruz walked the cast through the next inspired scene. Melonie would pretend to argue with her political lover. They would kiss and make up. up. The kiss would evolve into that standby of any porn film—thc blow job.

The director was a real genius, Mick thought. Another Fellini in the making.

The ghost of Kennedy and the ghost of Marilyn Monroe crashed in a standing dry hump. Despite the resemblance to JFK, the actor was never referred to as anything other than "Chief." Cruz didn't want to take any chances with legal problems.

Marilyn backed the chief into a wide-armed easy chair. Her fluffy blond hair bounced with each kiss on his open-shirted chest as she made the descent to her knees. She unzipped him, gasped in a "gee whiz" tone, and then bobbed her head up and down. The chief shifted in his chair and lifted his hips. He planted his feet on the sides of her knees so he could arch his back.

Mick found himself caught up in the scene. It was impossible not to watch her. He thought about Melonie's constant rap on the acting art. She considered herself a method actress. What was her motivation for this scene? Mick wondered. Patriotism?

Peter Cruz crawled on the floor. He motioned for the first cameraman to move in for a close-up of Melonie. "Okay, sugar," he urged. "Make it tasteful. This is a classy film." He tagged the air over his head. The second cameraman zoomed in on the chief's face. His head lolled from side to side.

Two minutes passed. "Hold back, chief," Cruz said. "Speed it up, Melonie. Hold back, hold back, chief. We want some tension here. Keep the audience wondering. Is he, or isn't he? Can the most beautiful sex goddess in the world satisfy the most powerful man in America?"

"Yes!" The chief shouted and straightened out like a man going into an epileptic fit. It was standard practice for orgasms to be visible, a tradition that had to be followed. The softcore version would be edited, but the hardcore had to have a long, spurting ejaculation.

That was where the "special effects" came in. Barbara stood by with a squirt gun in her hand. It was filled with a mixture of egg whites and milk of magnesia. If by some chance the cameras missed the orgasm or it wasn't real enough, she would spray the substance onto the actress.

"We got what we needed," Cruz said. He waved Barbara away. The actor collapsed. Melonie stood up and wrapped a white satin robe around her shoulders.

"You were great!" the chief said.

"Wonderful," Cruz agreed. "It's a beautiful scene. Power meets glamour and melts in its mouth. Good symbolism, Melonie. Okay, everybody, take ten."

Melonie chatted with the other actresses. She acted like she'd just done Shakespearean drama. Mick sat on the love seat by the primary entrance to the suite and stared at Melonie. What the hell went on inside her head?

Barbara dropped her water pistol on a table near the door and sat next to Mick. "When do you get off?" she asked. She crossed her legs and eased into the love seat. Her left hand patted the cushioned arm. Her right hand poised in the air looking for a place to land.

"When the man says," Mick answered. He nodded his head at Dartanian who was cornering Peter Cruz.

"Oh," she said. "Maybe we'll get off together."

He shook his head and laughed. There, was no escaping the subject with these girls. They all spoke in double entrendres. They viewed the world through carnal-colored glasses. Sex was a tunnel they lived in and never stepped out of. Barbara was a former porn star trying to make the switch to the other side of the camera. She craved respect and believed that sooner or later the straight world would call her. She was just like the other porn actresses, Mick thought. Barbara would mine fool's gold for the rest of her life.

She skimmed her fingers over his chest. Mick caught them in a fist that looked like a bear's paw compared to her small hand. He returned the hand to her lap. "I believe this is yours," he said.

Barbara laughed and shook her head. "You know, someday you're going to regret this. You're gonna think about me and what you missed out on."

"You're probably right," Mick said.

"And you'll find yourself saying 'What an idiot I was!' "

"It won't be the first time."

The redhead nodded. "But that's all right. Because one day you'll find me at your door to give you a second chance."

Mick wondered if he really had this effect on her or if she was just crazy. Since his first day on the set she had come on to him nonstop. Maybe it was because he was such a change from her usual crowd. Unlike the porn actors with their wavy styled coiffures and their flashy threads, Mick wore his brown hair in a short cut that barely touched his ears. He wore conservative suits and never saw the need to develop the ultra-cool rap all the young dudes around town affected. He was a no-nonsense man, which probably seemed exotic to Barbara.

"I know what's wrong," Barbara said. "You just don't like movies or the people who make them."

"Me?" He was shocked. "I stay up until five in the morning to watch *The Tenth Victim*, and you tell me I don't like movies! I love movies. Real ones, anyway."

"What's that movie about? I never heard of it."

"It's about agents and war games and Ursula Andress," he said.

"Ohhhh," she said. "So that's what you like. . . ."

Dartanian enjoyed listening to Peter Cruz. The writer-director of *Starlet* had no illusions about his livelihood. He made pornography. If critics wanted to label it art so they wouldn't feel guilty about watching it, that was their business.

Cruz battled with a stubborn cigar. He lit it four times before swearing and tossing it into an ashtray.

It burned slow and steady, daring him to pick it up again. "It's not my day, man," Cruz said. He leaned forward in his soft chair by the front window. "All these precautions are getting to me."

"Sure it's a pain in the ass," Dartanian said. "But without precautions, the hitters will get to you."

He nodded. "You were asking about Melonie's chances of making it in the real world."

"She seems to think she's going to be the next Marilyn Monroe for real. Hollywood's just waiting for her."

"Yeah," Cruz said. "Her and twenty thousand others like her. I say she doesn't make it outside of porn. But I won't tell her that. She's nice and that's unusual. Most of the chicks I work with have a giant set of knockers and a pair of brass balls. Melonie's different."

Dartanian peered through the Bushnell binoculars at the street below. Everything was in place. There was the station wagon on the hotel side of the street. Across from that was the silver LeSabre. He picked out Sin Simara walking the street in his aimless shuffle. The Japanese man window-shopped and shuffled down the sidewalk. He appeared to be in a fog, but Dartanian knew that Simara had every soul and every car on the block memorized. Like the other agents, he was just waiting for the wrong pattern to appear.

He put the binoculars on the ledge and tapped out a Pall Mall. It was his fourth of the day, and it was only two o'clock. One more and his quota would be filled. Maybe around midnight, he'd have the last one, sitting in the ICE house with a dark beer. "Some girls make it," he said. "From what I understand, TV has its share of actresses who started out in porn."

"True," Cruz said. "Some actresses will hump an elephant to make it to the top. But they never admit it when they get there. A girl lands a role in a dimwit comedy with a 44 share, and all of a sudden she forgets about those porn loops she did when she was nineteen or twenty. But, the ones who make it to TV are the ones who hide their past the best. Melonie is just too visible to make it. She's branded for the rest of her life as a beautiful, highly talented slut."

Dartanian exhaled a stream of smoke. "Why doesn't Melonie see all this?"

"That asshole Wilson put the blinds on her. Five years ago, she might have made the switch, but he kept her in the business, telling her that when she makes it to the top here she can write her own ticket to the straight flicks. By the way, thanks for banning him from the set."

"It was a pleasure," Dartanian said. And a necessity, he thought. Drew Wilson couldn't spend a day without calling attention to himself. He would jeopardize the security measures designed to trap the assassins.

Wilson had claimed to develop the *Starlet* package from the beginning. Dartanian found out in one day that the deal originated from the Taplin Corporation. Barry Leiderman, the Taplin exec in charge of the project, spelled out the deal to Dartanian. Taplin was moving into the video production and distribution field, anticipating it as the dominant gold mine of the future. Barry worked with three of his designers who specialized in developing storyboards for video games and came up with *Starlet* as a full-blown concept. He demanded Melonie Grand as the main actress and Peter Cruz as the writer-director. Drew Wilson entered the deal as excess baggage, a leech on Melonie's flesh.

Dartanian kept Cruz talking. The man knew his business, and he added a hands-on touch that no amount of research or dossiers could duplicate. "So there's no way Melonie can write her ticket," he said.

"She can make a lot of money in sexploitation flicks, but that's all. Look what happened to stars who just had mild stuff in their background. The stories I could tell. . . ."

"Please do," Dartanian said.

It took a week for Melonie to adapt to the safe house on East 9th Street. By then she acted like she'd lived there forever. It was a comfortable brownstone just off First Avenue in a neighborhood going upscale.

Behind the Early American furnishings of the first-floor bedrooms, library, and dining room was a 21st-century technology. Ultrasonic beams crisscrossed every room, set to activate a small computer monitor if any of the beams were broken. The computer then switched on a score of microchip transmitters embedded throughout the first floor. Hidden cameras with lenses coated to match the color of the walls were also activated. The cameras fed their images to a master control room on the third floor.

The second floor of the brownstone was set to release CN gas if an intruder made it that far. The apple blossom scent of the CN gas would dull the intruder a second before his eyes and lungs were temporarily knocked out.

Melonie lived on the third floor. She was unaware of the elaborate precautions that Dartanian had built into the house. But she was still calm and safe. The presence of so many armed men on the third floor had a tendency to relax her. For psychological reasons more than anything else, a fortress room was situated behind Melonie's bedroom. Reinforced walls, a steel door, and a battery-operated radio phone for outside communication were standard in a fortress room. The chances of anyone ever having to use the room were slim, but it was nice to have around.

The fourth floor of the building was wired like the first floor. In addition, Dartanian had installed sound alarms in each room. Set at the right frequency, the infrasonic sound waves could turn brains to mush.

The safe house was like a giant Venus flytrap. If the wrong fly entered, it might never come out again. Aside from protecting the client, whoever manned the third-floor control room could turn the entire house into an offensive weapon.

Melonie was escorted from the safe house for the location shootings at the Fairfax Hotel and for her media appearances. Dartanian had changed the agenda for all of the scheduled interviews, often keeping the reporter in the dark until the last minute.

Melonie appeared on three New York newscasts and had a ten-minute spot on *Midnight*, a syndicated entertainment show on cable. Every appearance was videotaped on a recorder in a room adjoining her bedroom in the safe house. She gave interviews to reporters from the *News, Post, Voice,* and a half-dozen men's magazines. Occasionally, the interviews took place at an apartment, but for the most part they were carried out in an armored

ICE vehicle. The reporters enjoyed the cloak and dagger aspect, although they would have preferred a public place like a bar or restaurant. The best part about being a reporter was being seen with the stars.

Melonie's appearance on the *Morris O'Donnell Show* was an unannounced surprise for the studio audience. That allowed Dartanian plenty of time to set up the security. Sprinkled throughout the predominantly middle-aged female crowd were several burly DSS agents. Val Wagner, the sole female ICE agent sat in the front row. Her long black hair and pleasing figure were hidden by a gray wig and a shapeless flower-print dress.

The *Morris O'Donnell Show* was an hour-long program filmed in New York and carried by hundreds of stations across the United States. He specialized in controversial subjects designed to titillate and outrage his low-brow audience. Melonie was perfect for the show. Women loved to hate her.

On the Thursday night before her next scheduled filming at the Fairfax, Melonie reviewed the tapes of her appearances. It was a welcome change of pace to watch herself wearing clothes and talking like a genuine human being, instead of steaming the camera with a smorgasboard of sex.

"This is Karen Atwood for *Action News* at an undisclosed location in Manhattan." The chirpy reporter on the videotape gave the camera her best somber look. Her Goldilocks curls bounced constantly, since she nodded her head with every word. "I'm speaking with Melonie Grand, the well-known porn star who narrowly escaped death in the Porn Massacre just two weeks ago." The camera panned the main lobby of the Fairfax. "Melonie tells us that she is not going to back down, that she is going to complete *Starlet.*"

Melonie's image flashed just long enough for her to say, "I'm not going to back down. It's a tragedy, but I can't let my life be ruled by fear."

"Melonie, there are rumors that your entourage includes a number of armed men who escort you around town. Is that true?"

Melonie laughed. "There are hundreds of rumors about me. But that's the first time I ever heard anything about armed men. As I said, I'm not going to change my lifestyle for anyone."

The videotape went blank.

Melonie sat cross-legged on the floor, unconsciously doing the yoga exercises that kept her shape in shape over the last ten years. She smiled and thought of the interview with Karen Atwood. Even while she denied being escorted by armed men, one of the cameramen focusing on the entrance to the Fairfax had been on guard. She had seen the inside of the dummy camera on the tripod. Inside the metal casing was a US M3 submachine gun. During the briefing, Dartanian had explained the defensive wall that would be around her at all times. The man with the camera had called it a "greasegun." She remembered how the DSS agent spoke of the weapon with something close to affection in his voice. These men were really "out there," she thought. Of course, she was glad to be in their company.

Melonie put another cartridge in the Sanyo video recorder. She sat back into a lotus position, relaxed her shoulders, and straightened her back. She clenched her fists and placed them palms up on her thighs. She clicked her teeth together several times at a slow pace to reduce the pace of her heartbeat, then went into her neck and chest exercises.

Two more newscasts came on the tape. Like the first, they showed several interiors of the Fairfax Hotel and one exterior shot. It wouldn't take an Einstein to figure out where the "undisclosed location" was. Dartanian was throwing out bait for the porn killers. Every day of filming was like an anticlamax. She half-expected to see a gun pointing at her head every time she stepped out of the Fairfax. That was the reason why she spent most of her free time doing exercises. To calm down. Waiting for a killer to strike did a number on her system.

A loud smack of applause from the videotape caught Melonie's attention. The *Morris O'Donnell Show* was on. He welcomed Melonie with his hands clasped together, rubbing them in joy like he was about to feed a Christian to the lions. O'Donnell cultivated a fatherly look with his perfectly cut silver hair and his wide-rimmed black glasses. He gave the impression that anything you told him would be a secret between the two of you—never mind the millions of viewers.

"Melonie is here to tell us about her life as a porn star. First off, Melonie, if I'm not wrong, you do enjoy making those horrible sex films. Is that correct?"

"It's given me a lot of exposure," Melonie said.

The expected laugh came when Morris rolled his eyes to the audience and said, "I'll say." After a few minutes of harmless questions, he came back to his favorite theme. He got up from the cozy chair facing hers and stood at the edge of the stage. He pointed at her like a prosecuting attorney nailing a murderer in front of a jury. "That woman over there—excuse me, I should say girl, she's so young—that woman makes her living by performing perverted sexual acts with male and female porno stars. But she doesn't see anything wrong with it." Morris scratched his head. "I think something's wrong here. Is it me or is it her?"

Before the audience had a chance to respond, Morris closed in on Melonie. "Don't you feel shame? Don't you feel cheap? I know this is the twentieth century, but *come on*! What do you think, audience? Give me some help out there!"

The audience mooed like a giant cow. Angry housewives shouted their disgust, a few feminists denounced Melonie as a traitor, and the DSS agents laughed.

Morris spent the rest of the hour soliciting juicy stories from Melonie, only to condemn them a moment later. He hardly mentioned the murder attempt, but when he did, he managed to convey that the porn stars deserved their fate.

The man was such an obvious panderer, Melonie thought. But he reached millions of homes and he was good for publicity. She remembered how he visited her backstage after roasting her for sixty minutes.

"Doing anything tonight?" he asked.

A sultry smiled appeared on her lips as she approached the door. She whispered, "No," and shut it in his face.

Four

"We go down in five minutes," Dartanian announced to Melonie and Craig Patroon, her DSS guard in the Fairfax Hotel.

"Oh?" Melonie purred. She was breathless and beautiful in a tight white skirt and matching top. A red sash hung from her waist with ties flapping midway down her skirt.

"Down to the street," Dartanian said.

"Ohhhh," Melonie said. "How dreary."

Peter Cruz and Barbara struck the set for the day's filming. The Kennedy clone and a top-heavy brunette sat on a long white sofa breathing like boxers between rounds. They were exhausted from the last scene. Cruz had demanded several takes before he was satisfied with their performance. Two impatient cameramen paced the suite.

The *Starlet* group would be taken down to street level ten minutes after Melonie was driven away. Dartanian's escort team worked on a one-target basis. Melonie could be moved quicker and safer without the confusion caused by taking the porn crew all at once. Too many untrained bodies got in the way.

"How do you feel?" Dartanian asked.

"Scared," Melonie said. "I'm always scared to go out."

"Do what I say and there's nothing to worry about."

"You're the man," Melonie said. "Your wish is my command." Her long lashed eyes tossed him another come-on.

The porn actress had become infatuated with him. It wasn't the first time a woman fell for Dartanian while under his protection. It was a common situation. Patty Hearst ended up marrying her bodyguard, as did a hundred other less publicized socialites. Dependence on a bodyguard often turned to adoration and slavish devotion. Women weren't used to seeing knights in the twentieth century. They especially weren't used to having a man like Dartanian watch over them day and night, ready to put his life on the line at any moment. It was a heady experience.

Dartanian played down her invitations. As a professional, he wasn't about to take advantage of her vulnerable state of mind. Besides, she wasn't his type. Melonie cloaked her personality in too many Hollywood veils. He liked real women, not phantasms born in an X-rated factory.

He nodded to Patroon. A former pistol instructor for the State Police, Patroon had spent two years as a DSS man. He was in line for ICE, unknowingly winding his way through the selection process. Patroon left the suite to signal two waiting DSS agents that it was time to sweep the hall. The radio man notified the street cars that Dartanian was coming down in a few minutes.

An armored Continental Mark VI glided to the curb in front of the Fairfax. Behind it came the real transport car, a plain looking Datsun 810 sedan.

The Continental was there as a decoy to ride interference for the Datsun. Both vehicles had double-glazed, bullet-resistant glass and lightweight, ceramic and plastic armor more effective than traditional steel plating. The armor encased the entire passenger compartment in a safety cocoon with hidden gun ports at each door.

Two more support vehicles waited on the street. Mick Porter sat in a gimmicked Country Squire parked on the same side as the hotel. The station wagon's reinforced ramming bumper faced the canopied entrance.

Sitting in a LeSabre, directly across from the Fairfax, was Tim Reed. The deceptively thin ICE agent was six-foot-six. He had red hair and a boyish face that had never worn a beard. He looked more like a gawky kid trying out for a basketball team than an ICE man. Yet it was that same innocent face that led the naval assault from the St. Lawrence against the Montreal slavers. Reed's SEAL training worked wonders in the civilian sector.

Sin Simara continued patrolling the street in a hang-around shuffle. He looked like he had nothing on his mind but killing time.

Dartanian studied the street below one more time. He had a premonition. It was a brief glimpse into the future, a scent of blood on a summer breeze. There had been a tenseness in the air after each day of filming, a mute but shared dread of what might be waiting on the street. This time it was the real thing.

Alex put down the binoculars. There was no sign of an enemy, but he was sure the bait had been taken. Melonie's appearances on television would have given away the filming location by now. If the killers were smart, they could scout the street and avoid detection. Assassins or psychopaths, they would strike. Dartanian's senses reached out. He drifted into that state of alertness where every movement and every word seemed to be in slow motion.

"I'm going to fall down," Melonie said. "My knees are shaking!" She stomped her feet and wrapped her arms around her chest. "Dammit!" she hissed. "I feel like such a jerk. I don't want to go out there."

"Nothing's going to happen," Dartanian said. "Relax."

Melonie nodded and did what had the most calming effect on herself. She paraded to a wall mirror and fluffed her hair. Reflex took over. She rolled a tube of red lipstick over her mouth, blinked her eyes to check her lashes, and smiled into the mirror. She looked like she was going to a party.

Dartanian checked the clip in the Skorpion. If anything, it was going to be a theme party. And the theme was death.

Mick Porter tapped the accelerator. The supercharged Country Squire pulsed with power. The solid engine was tuned to a quiet hum. He glanced in the rear-view mirror for a look at the street behind. Nothing unusual was happening.

Up the Street, Tim Reed turned his head toward the Fairfax. Any moment now, Dartanian would appear. Mick was glad to be down here where there was room to move without peeling Barbara from his body. That woman unsettled him.

"One minute till show time," the radio chattered. Mick glanced at the fifth floor window where Jack Williamson manned the street watch.

He flicked a switch on the dash. It made a buzz no louder than a push-button window. A red light blinked between the left and right turn signals. It too was a signal: the battle wagon was ready to ride. Behind the right headlight was a modified Thompson submachine gun. The model 1928 was mounted above the wheel well and separated from the engine by a steel wall. Ventilation holes dotted the right fender. Mick could fire a 50-round drum of .45 ACP ammo with another flick of the switch.

The setup was as legal as a $30 bill, but ICE wasn't in the sainthood business. The Tommy was a perfect passenger. It spoke only when it had to.

Mick doubted he would use the Thompson. He'd activated the switch by habit, just as he did the other days he worked on the street. His Ingram M10 rested on his lap with a 20-round clip.

"Thirty seconds till show time."

Sin Simara cruised West 49th Street with his hands in his loose pants pockets. The tight black T-shirt showed a lot of lean muscle, but he didn't look dangerous. Navigator sunglasses hid his eyes. He'd let his thin mustache grow until it was shaggy like the hair that hung down his neck. The normally clean-cut Simara had been working on a DEA coke bust. He kept the shaggy look after the bust went down, because it fit the current ICE operation so well. He looked like a dealer or a street type waiting for a scene to happen.

No matter how innocuous he looked, Simara was a potent weapon. He carried a dozen shurikens in his cloth belt but rarely used the throwing stars. Simara preferred the control of hand-to-hand combat. If he could reach out and touch a man, that man was as good as dead.

The slender Japanese agent could transform his fingers into steel claws and his toes into ice picks. Unlike the martial artists that used the balls of the feet for front kicks, Simara adapted the Uechi technique of conditioning the toes until they were strong enough to use as striking points. Bare toes that could smash cement blocks to powder could blast a man's insides apart with a roundhouse or a front snap kick.

He stopped in front of a bakery window that offered bagels, French bread, and the reflection of Mick Porter sitting in his war wagon.

Two men in their forties walked in a lockstep pattern. They kept their eyes straight ahead. Mick studied them when they reached a spot across the street from his station wagon. Both wore cheap suits and affected the style of important business men. So did a million other men in New York City. Every day was a contest to see who could look the most important, walk the fastest, and talk the loudest. These two did okay in the fast-walk department but blew it when it came to looking the part of executives in a hurry. Mick figured them to be shoe salesmen or clerks. Since they were heading away from the Fairfax, he didn't give them any more thought—until Jack Williamson's SOS boomed from the radio.

"This could be it!" Williamson warned. "We've got repeat customers in a white Chevy Impala. They've rounded the corner and double-parked about 40 yards behind Mick. They're waiting for somebody. They're handling some kind of hardware in the car. Okay, here's the lineup. Two men in front. Two men climbing into the back seat."

Mick studied them in the mirror. He saw the

pair of cheap suiters get into the Impala. He pushed down on the brake and revved the engine. The wagon lurched like a bull pawing the dirt before a charge. Mick forced out the tightness inside with a long exhale.

"They're changing the lineup." Williamson spoke in a controlled roar. "The driver's staying. So is a man in the back seat. The other two are out of the car. They're packing heat and they ain't cops. Crossing to Mick's side of the street. *Shotgun*! I see a shotgun in the back seat. This is it, this is the hit!"

Mick waved two fingers to Simara, then pointed to the men coming on foot. Simara nodded. He backed into the alcove of the bakery.

The Impala rolled into light traffic. A chewed-up muffler groaned when it shot forward an instant later. Mick picked up the driver in his mirror and saw his lips tighten. A stocky man in the back seat inched the barrel of a Savage 77E shotgun out the window.

Melonie stepped from the hotel between Dartanian and Craig Patroon. The man with the shotgun just had to lift his elbow to splatter the porn actress with the pump-action weapon. Victory flashed on his face.

Mick floored the gas pedal and released the brake. The wagon shrieked into action. Wham! It speared the back left fender of the Impala. The nose of the Squire crunched through the metal as though it were aluminum foil.

The steering wheel whipped through the driver's fingers and nearly broke them. He screamed and held his hands in front of his contorted face.

Tires squealed on tar, as the wagon ripped up the road and pushed the Impala sideways down the street. Breaking glass and torn metal fell off the battling vehicles.

Mick's teeth cracked together when Tim Reed rammed the other side of the Impala. The driver bounced like a rag doll. He shouted to his gunner. The man in the back seat had gone blank with rage. When he came back to reality, he slit his mouth with a curse and jabbed the shotgun out the window.

Two blasts kicked the windshield to hell. Two huge pock marks imploded the bulletproof glass above the steering wheel. Mick had ducked and flicked the Thompson switch when the shotgun eyed him. He wasn't about to stare down a Savage, no matter how good the glass was.

The Thompson punched 50 rounds through the side of the Impala. The shotgunner looked surprised, then dead. His head danced on a spineless neck and sank out of sight.

Three shots from a Ruger .357 Magnum whacked into the hood of the Country Squire and chomped into the windshield. Mick left the wagon in gear and bailed out. He aimed the Big Mac on the run and was about to fire when the driver's face jumped off. Tim Reed had chopped him from the side with a full burst from his Ingram. The force of the 9mm slugs smacked the driver's head back against the window frame like a puppet-master just pulled his string.

Mick whirled toward the bakery with the Ingram M10 cradled in his arms.

Browning GP pistols came out of the jackets. Once the car battle started, there was no need to hide. The sidewalk hit team raced to the Fairfax like long-distance runners spotting the finish line.

The man in front had a crew cut and a maroon blazer. Except for the gun in his hand he might have been a gym teacher. His eyes were lit by glory. The car team was knocked out. It was up to him to pick up the baton.

A huffing man ran ten yards behind him. He was thin and pale in a loose suit that flapped in the breeze. The Browning GP hung awkwardly in his flailing hand. He was an amateur thrown into a gladiator's arena, but that didn't stop him from going for the kill.

The first man aimed the 13-round Browning shoulder high as he ran. His left hand whipped up and down, chugging the breath out of the 250-round locomotive. His right index finger pulled back on the trigger.

A lead pipe busted his throat. The cartilage split into a dozen shards. Before the pain got to him, the lead pipe grew a hand. The hand raked his eyes, slipped around the back of his neck, and tossed him head first into a wire trash barrel. He bounced off the barrel with a meshed wire imprint on his face. Hardly able to breathe, he crawled on the sidewalk and reached for his dropped pistol. The Browning was his last link to a life rapidly fading away.

The second man skidded to a stop. He'd seen a little Japanese man fly out of a bakery and whip his forearm at his partner's neck. A second later, the huge man was trashed and bleeding on the sidewalk.

He squeezed off a shot, missed, and stood in front of the Japanese wild man for a second try. He held the Browning in a two-handed grip and sighted on his face.

Sin Simara batted the gun away with a left

crescent kick. The blow spun the man around. He managed to hold onto the gun despite the numbness in his left hand. For that, he died. Simara used the momentum of the first kick to launch his second. He crouched low when his left foot landed, pivoted, and then crushed the man's skull with a spinning back kick. Simara's heel hit so hard that the man's feet lifted off the ground before he fell on his face.

Simara dropped to the sidewalk at the sound of staggering footsteps behind him. He rolled over to the edge of the curb and saw the burly man waving his pistol around. Blood streamed down his cheeks. He made strangling sounds as he walked forward like a creature from a nightmare. Bam! A 9mm Parabellum slug tore a chunk out of the sidewalk. Bam! The second shot struck three feet away from Simara. The man was firing blind. Simara silently rose from his crouch. The man wheeled toward him. The Browning fired again. Simara skipped forward to jump-kick the man out of his misery. The man aimed at the sound. It was a race between his trigger finger and Simara's foot.

The gun hopped out of his hand. The hand jerked in a splattering blur. A stitch of bullet holes dug a red trail up the man's arm to his chest.

Simara looked to his right and saw Mick Porter. He'd emptied a full clip into the man. Mick nodded his head and shoved another clip into the Ingram M10. Simara ran to the Fairfax where another pair of Mad Hatters materialized.

Alex Dartanian was midway to the Datsun when the hit teams struck. He shoved the small of Melonie's back with his left hand. The blow knocked her off her feet and propelled her face first into the back seat of the Datsun. *Turn left*, the thought. *Left*. That's where the next attack would come from. The first and second waves came from the right. The final wave would come from the opposite direction.

He zipped the Skorpion from his shoulder holster and spun in a circle. Dartanian caught a glimpse of Porter and Simara, then, as he completed the turn, he saw Craig Patroon's shocked face. Patroon tiptoed forward, pushed by a stream of bullets in his back. Even though he was guarding the left side, instinct made him turn to the action down the street. He toppled to the sidewalk stiff with agony.

Dartanian dove to the sidewalk. Three blasts from a 9mm automatic tore up the cement where he'd been standing. If Dartanian hadn't made the split-second decision to turn, he would have joined Patroon.

He followed the hit man who nailed Patroon with the sight of his Skorpion. The gray-haired man was in the act of swinging his Heckler and Koch VP70 back to Dartanian. The Continental Mark VI hopped the curb and smacked the man into the stone face of the Fairfax. He bounced forward. Dartanian wasted him with a swarm of 7.65mm stingers.

The second man crashed into the Continental. He fired a wild shot at Dartanian, then scrambled up the side of the car. His pistol hammered on the roof a second before his grinning face popped up. His greased hair stuck out at crazy angles. He no longer seemed to be aware of Dartanian.

He stood on the roof of the Continental. His pistol hung idly in his right hand. It was crazy.

The man had stopped fighting in the middle of his attack. The sight of Dartanian holding the Skorpion M61 on him didn't bother him at all.

"*Drop the gun!*" Dartanian shouted. "Now."

He came out of his dream and pointed his automatic in Dartanian's direction. Alex iced his gut with three rounds. The man shook his head no. He brought his pistol up again for another try. The man screamed like a banshee. Dartanian blasted him in the throat and turned the scream into a sick gurgling sound. The pistol bounced on the roof of the Continental.

The driver of the Continental looked at Dartanian for a signal. Dartanian stayed him with his left hand. His right held the smoking Skorpion.

What was this guy smiling about? There he was, teetering in and out of death's arms, and he was smiling. The disheveled and bullet-torn man acted like he was going to his reward a victor. Something kept him on his feet. Something powered him. What was it? Dartanian wondered. Love? Hate? Madness? The man reminded him of a dog he'd seen once. Hit by a car, the crushed and bleeding Shepherd dragged himself off the road to die on the grass. This man's grass was the Datsun. He looked at it and fumbled under his shirt with his right hand. At first, Dartanian thought he was holding his wounds. Then he saw the man tugging at a bulky shape beneath his shirt at chest level.

Sonofabitch, Dartanian thought. He guessed the man's secret just as he dove off the Continental.

"*Bomb!*" Dartanian shouted. He dropped the Skorpion and threw his hands overhead to catch the dying man. "Uhhhhh!" he groaned when the weight nearly wrenched his arms out of their sockets. He spun at a crazy angle with the man's momentum and dangled him over the sidewalk. Streaks of blood gushed onto Dartanian's face and hands. "He's wired!" Dartanian shouted to Sin Simara who ran to his side.

Simara nodded. He rapped the Datsun three times and motioned the driver forward. The silver LeSabre darted in front of it to ride interference. The Continental backed off the curb and sealed the trail of the motorcade.

There was no time to disarm the bomb. The man had activated the timer. It could be ten, thirty, or sixty seconds at the longest. It could be an impact bomb with a delayed detonator. It could go off any time.

Simara ran to the middle of the street and yanked open the back door of the Impala. Mick jumped into the station wagon and screeched down the street in reverse. Dartanian hauled the carcass to the Impala and dropped it on top of the dead shotgunner. He turned with Simara and raced from the car.

They made it halfway to the sidewalk on foot. The concussion from the bomb flew them the rest of the way. Dartanian rolled when he hit the cement. Dragon breath seared his heels. Simara bounced on top of him. Then he too rolled away from the flames that jetted out of the Chevy windows.

The echo of the explosion was deafening, like a dozen thunderclaps hammered into one blast. The men inside the Impala were blown through the roof. The parts that stayed inside were incinerated.

Cinders, metal rain, and human bone fragments dropped from a dark gray cloud above the Chevy crematorium.

Dartanian looked at the fallen Craig Patroon. Soldiers die in every war, he thought. So do friends.

He got to his feet. That strange elation that came from battle was stifled into silence by sorrow for Patroon's death.

"We've seen these kind of faces before," Simara said. "That was a suicide squad. They were willing to die for someone."

"You ask me," Dartanian said, "that someone is a fucking lunatic."

Five

Every prophet worth a damn had a vision. Luke Revere had his two or three times a week. It was always the same. A shimmering blue halo enveloped his trim six-foot frame. Then came the enchantment, brilliant white, beckoning, and all-consuming.

The vision was Melonie Grand. She appeared to him on a wide screen that dropped from the chapel ceiling. Revere watched the X-rated apparition from a black lectern studded with videotape controls. Flickering images bounced from his Johnny Carson suit back to the glowing screen. They meshed with the milky white flesh of Melonie Grand and splayed over him once again. It was the deepest communion he'd ever felt.

"You sinner," Luke whispered. "You beautiful sinner." It was three in the afternoon, almost time for the next Ministry of the Air broadcast. The studio audience was a well-dressed menagerie of WASPs and fundamentalists who loved money and hated Commies. They also hated humanists. They hated anything Luke Revere told them to hate.

All *real* Christians knew that Commies and humanists were behind welfare, inflation, abortion, evolution, pornography, and crime. They also knew that God especially liked white people, a few blacks, and Congressmen on the Ministry's list of Correct Legislators. Everybody else had better watch out.

A rap on the chapel door startled him. "You're on in ten minutes, Mr. Revere." He rapped several more times. "Mr. Revere?"

"Thank you," he said. He tossed down three fingers of gin. "I'll be ready." He dropped onto a padded leather swivel chair behind the lectern.

Melonie Grand's image flooded him with sensory overload. She hung there in gigantic proportions, going down. Her expert touch fluttered over the stiff member, while her drinking kisses coaxed out a splashy orgasm. After a lengthy close-up of her bobbing head, the camera zoomed in on the man's pleasure-wracked face. The man was Luke Revere.

The film was ten years old, a grainy porno loop revived and transferred to videotape. Melonie was eighteen at the time. Revere was twenty-six then, but didn't look out of his teens.

He'd been a small-time tent preacher who hadn't mastered the racket yet. He made his real money as a jam auctioneer with a carnival that traveled up and down the East Coast. At the time, he used his real name, Tim Lockwood.

One summer night, he preached to a tiny audience on the edge of the carnival grounds. There he met Melonie Grand. He'd been thinking of giving up the salvation biz and was an easy mark for the temptress. He didn't give a damn what happened that night. Ten years and sixteen million followers later, that wicked night threatened to ruin everything.

Like the videotapes he was addicted to, Luke

Revere's memory whirred into reverse, jumped into fast-forward, and spliced together the high points of his multimillion dollar movement.

Six stray cats drifted into the musty tent to kill time with the young preacher. Two were elderly ladies who thought God was where you found him, even on the outskirts of a carnival working Boston, Massachusetts. One man was there to find salvation, a hot meal, and a place to sleep.

The other three were there for kicks. Two men with beards and bell bottoms accompanied a beautiful hippie chick. They wore denims studded with peace patches. She wore a tie-dyed T-shirt that stretched over her breasts like a second skin. A blue headband pulled back her ass-length blond hair. Crackling white vinyl boots hugged her calves.

It was the fading days of hippiedom. The dying gods of psychedelia had joined forces to create one last gasp of reckless beauty. Her name was Melonie.

Revere delivered an awkward and unpolished spiel that evening. He had a hard time concentrating on anything else but Melonie's T-shirt. Salvation ran a close second but lost out to her prize bust. The usually hot air under the canvas had turned into a brutal heat wave. Mosquitoes and black flies attacked the audience. They left one by one, even as he preached.

One elderly lady said, "Keep at it, son. There's something in you." She and her friend walked hand in hand out of the tent. That left Revere with the hippie chick and one of the bearded freaks.

"I gotta split," the freak said. "This ain't my trip."

"So split," she said.

He hooked his thumbs into tissue-thin jeans,

smirked at Revere, and shuffled out into the open air.

Revere preached for another minute before he gave up the ghost. He stared at Melonie. She'd kicked her feet up over the back of a folding chair and slouched in her seat. The way she busted out of her T-shirt and cutoffs reminded him of one of the girls from *L'il Abner*.

"Why are *you* still around?" he asked.

She stared him down. "I always wanted to ball a preacher."

It hit him like a ton of stripper's feathers. He felt a pounding in his heart and his groin. "You're confused, child," he counseled.

Melonie laughed. "Offer expires in sixty seconds. Save that child crap for the marks."

"What's this about?"

"I already told you, man. I've been watching, you know. You turn me on, and like I said, I always wanted to bang a preacher. Even if he is a fake."

Was this some kind of trap? he thought. He pictured a group of people standing outside the tent listening to them. But what would be the point? Still, it couldn't hurt to be on the safe side. "The world needs to resist temptation," he said.

She said, "Bye." She stood and turned on her heels.

"The world also needs no-bullshit women like you."

They went to a motel in Boston where four studio apartments served as communal headquarters for a tribe of city hippies. Revere's straight threads clashed with the freak-chic clothes of the hippies. But he didn't mind. He fit in where it counted.

Melonie had seen a kindred spirit in him. She took him for a hustler and teased him about his act.

He relaxed and partied with them. After two hours, ten bottles of wine, and a half-ounce of grass, they became life-long friends. Revere met a relatively straight-looking man who worked as a cameramen for a local TV station. The man gave Melonie some coke.

"Try some," Melonie urged. "Things go better with coke."

It was the key to the club. He tried coke and entered the clique. He found out that the cameraman made porno films on the side. Melonie was his favorite actress. She beat the system by acting in porn films to work her way through college. Why bust her ass for nickles and dimes when she could make a fortune having a ball?

It sounded logical to Revere.

The hippies paired off. Some tripled off. Luke Revere, who thought he was pretty hip because he'd made it with a few carnival strippers, found himself at his first orgy.

He also found himself staring at a camera while Melonie went down on him. For a split second, he thought of calling off the show. But Melonie was from another world, and he wanted in. The preacher business was a bust. No one took him seriously. He would probably give it up and concentrate on the jam auctions. What the hell difference did it make what he did tonight? Nobody else seemed to mind the camera.

His wine-soaked brain took over. He let the camera capture him and Melonie. He even took a turn filming some of his new soul mates. It was a gas.

The failed preacher was among friends, doing

what they were doing. What could come of it? No big deal, he thought. For one night, he was a fucking movie star.

That night stayed with him over the years. It was a skeleton in his closet that jangled louder with each new triumph. Luke Revere's Ministry became a high-volume business, due to his carny training at manipulating audiences.

His body cuaght up to his age. The thin face filled out with strong cheeks and a sharp jaw. When he was thirty, the natural build of an athlete fell on him like a gift from heaven. He wore his hair in the Kirk Douglas style of the Fifties and Sixties that people associated with authority figures.

The child was gone. In his place stood a man capable of preaching to crowds without making them uncomfortable. His voice changed into a deep rumble fit to deliver the Word. He picked the name Luke Revere because it sounded holy and trustworthy. He wrapped it with a Reverend title, plucked out of thin air just as the other TV evangelists had. Of all the reverends and ministers who worked the TV con game, only one of them had actually been ordained by an honest-to-God organized religion. Revere considered the rest of the "reverends" as legitimate and sacred as a pack of rats' assholes. He was among his peers.

He owed his success to a deep faith in American gullibility and his experience with the carnival. When he'd been a jam auctioneer, he milked crowds by taking them on a guilt trip. He gave free gold-plated pens and cigarette lighters to everyone in the audience who raised their hands. These became the "elite." Only they were eligible to bid on his stock.

Within twenty minutes, he had them convinced he was a naive salesman who didn't know the value of his products, although the cheap stuff he handed out never totaled more than twenty dollars. The elite felt guilty over fleecing such a sweet but dumb salesman. Since they psychologically believed they owed him something, they were in a mood to buy. Consequently, they bid up to $20 for a two-dollar camera, $60 for a TV that cost half that, and $15 for a $1.98 Swiss watch.

The innocent but dumb auctioneer made a fortune.

Revere used the same technique when he jumped into the preacher business full time. He triggered audience guilt by telling them they weren't doing enough to spread the Word. *He* was. *He* would do it for them. Luke Revere would carry their burden of witnessing the gospel on his shoulders. But he couldn't do it without money. However, if they saw fit to support the Ministry, why God would reward them. God understood they were busy. That's why God sent Luke Revere to spread the Word. A contribution to Luke's Ministry was a contribution to God.

Luke gave them the gospel they wanted to hear. Christians *could* buy their way into heaven. On top of their weekly donations, they could buy double-blessed crucifixes for only $30 that would show God they really cared. They could buy special prayers guaranteed to reach God because Luke Revere would say them himself. It was a bargain-basement church, and it was crowded.

Revere prospered. The tent preachings grew into lofty crusades. He preached to county fair crowds and packed stadiums. His old carny wanderlust drove him across America with an evangelical road show every summer. He married a sweet wife named Peggy, with the figure of a Playboy bunny and the heart of a barracuda. She sang psalms and twittered next to her holy husband on stage. She was 38-24-38 TNT packed into a high-necked white dress. God bless Luke. God bless Peggy. God bless us all. Luke was in a brand new carnival.

The Ministry grew like a mutant strain gone wild in a sea of American credulity. The Ministry of the Air beamed into millions of homes by satellite. Luke Revere bought an abandoned seminary in White Plains and restored it as Ministry headquarters. He held weekly evangelical conferences and invited clergy from New York City and White Plains itself. But the theologians along Seminary Row in White Plains ignored him like he was white trash. He was million-dollar trash, but trash just the same. Reverend Soames, a black New York preacher, was the only one who paid a call.

The snubs didn't bother Luke Revere. He had the audience that counted. He found paradise, and it was right here in America. Many Americans didn't like to think. They liked to be told what to do. Television had conditioned them well and softened them for the evangelist blitz of the Eighties. Praise God, America was the only country on earth where it was possible to sell Wheaties and God through the same media.

The Ministry of the Air and its subsidiaries took in $62 million a year. Revere was almost on a par with the other TV shills. Soon he would surpass them.

He knew that his dream was at hand. The only thing that could cause it to slip through his fingers was the nightmare. Melonie Grand came to him in his sleep. And though the chances were extremely slim—after all he had changed his name—he feared discovery more than anything. If word got out about the film, his empire would fall.

He pushed the fear out of his head with coke and alcohol and everything that money could buy. He had almost convinced himself that it had never happened, that it was all just a bad dream.

Until Ralph Hendricks showed up with the nightmare in his pocket.

After each Sunday service, Luke Revere held court in his chapel. He met his congregation one at a time and shared faith with them. He listened to their problems, counseled them, and joked with them. No matter how boring or inane the conversation, Luke chatted with them. In his eyes, they were all equal. Fools, every one of them. In their eyes, he was a man of God who had time for all.

Ralph Hendricks didn't look like a regular when he stepped into the chapel. He wasn't wearing a jacket or a tie. His shirt was crumpled, and the tails stuck out of his belt. A bald tire track ran down the center of his head. If the tufts of hair on either side were a bit longer, he could have been Bozo the Clown on a bad day.

He eased into a soft-backed folding chair across from Revere. Before speaking, he double-checked the room to make sure they were alone.

"Mr. Revere?"

Revere nodded. "What can I do for you?"

"I'm a film editor."

"Oh?" Revere warmed to him. "The Ministry is always looking for volunteers."

"That figures. Anyway, I got something you should see." He bit his lip and folded his arms over his chest.

Revere became excessively calm. Despite the ice that creeped up his spine and the dryness in his throat, he smiled and bombed the man with love. Ralph Hendricks was invulnerable.

He shook his head in a way that scolded Revere. Then, like a solemn co-conspirator, Hendricks reached into the pocket of a hooded sweatshirt folded over his lap. "Here," he said. He passed a black videotape cartridge to Revere. "It's VHS. I figure you got a videotape machine, right? After all, this *is* a TV studio."

Revere stared at the tape. It was labeled *M.G.* "What is it?" he asked. It had to be Melonie Grand.

"Play it and find out if you have to. But look, pal, we both know what it is. It's you and a broad doing the deed, man. Know what I'm talking about?"

He drummed his fingers over the cartridge. "There are more people waiting out there. I have to see them."

"How long's it gonna take?"

"About half an hour."

"I'll wait. Then you and me can do business." He backed out of the chapel. "I'm a reasonable man. You'll see."

Revere sweated through the remaining visitors, but he didn't show it. It was against the Revere image to show weakness. When the last visitor left, Revere summoned the film editor. He didn't have to see the tape to know what was on it.

"How did you know it was me?" Revere asked.

"I watch you for kicks sometimes. You're better than Archie Bunker."

"The tape," Revere said. "How did you get it?"

Ralph Hendricks explained his work as a porn editor and occasional filmmaker. A man he knew was gathering old films of Melonie Grand for reissue on videotape as porn classics. Hendricks had already sold him a few reels of early Melonie when he stumbled onto the black-and-white film that featured her and Revere.

"At first, I thought it was kinda funny," Hendricks said. "But when I transferred the film to videotape I was stricken by an inspiration from above. Instead of the $300 I stood to get, I figured a gentleman like you would be even more generous."

"How generous?"

"Twenny grand. One price buys all. If not, I gotta package of dupes all set to deliver. You dig?"

This was the end of his church. It didn't take a Martin Luther. All it took was a sleazy Ralph Hendricks. "You've done the right thing in coming here," Revere said. "You'll get what you seek." He stood, overwhelmed by sadness. Tears came to his eyes as he staggered to a small altar in the corner.

"Come on, man! It ain't *that* bad."

"God sent you here as my punishment. A signal that I need redemption. I will pay you, but first, will you join me in prayer?"

"Sure," he said. "If that's what it takes."

Ralph Hendricks knelt at a gold railing before the altar. Revere bowed once toward the altar, then turned and clasped his hands in prayer over his head. "Pray with me, brother."

Hendricks bowed his head.

Revere slammed his meaty fists on the kneeling man's head. Hendricks grunted and slumped over the railing. Revere caved in the skull with another blow from the clasped prayer hands. He pressed his neck flat against the railing and strangled the parasite who dared to blackmail a man of the cloth.

Two hours later, he stepped into Hendricks' apartment at St. Mark's Place in the East Village. It looked more like an electronic repair shop than a place to live. Television and stereo sets with their innards hanging out cluttered two shelves in the living room. The dining room served as a small studio with screens and props at one side of the room, while monitors, editing consoles, and projectors filled the other.

Luke Revere took his time. He left the apartment with a carton full of 8mm reels and videotapes.

The chapel vibrated from an onslaught of cathedral music. Somber organ chords yanked Revere back to the present. He had two minutes before he was due on stage. He flicked off the Melonie Grand videotape that had started it all, then checked himself in the mirror. He combed his hair, straightened his brown suit, then opened the combination lock on a tall safe behind the altar. Inside were a dozen heavy metal crucifixes and an oval tin of white powder.

Revere cut two lines of coke on a gold plate and sniffed twice. He always coked up just before a television appearance. The Big C stood for charisma.

A key turned in the chapel door. Revere turned to see Deacon Archer duck under the doorway. Something was wrong. Archer and the other deacons weren't due back for another day.

"What are you doing here?"

"They fucked up," Deacon Archer said. "Dead. Every one of them." The one-time biker stood with his arms at his sides. He wore a gray surgeon's shirt with a V neck and notched short sleeves. Even with his arms at rest, his biceps were swollen.

A matching set of tattooed railroad spikes ran down his muscle-chopped forearms.

Deacon Archer had short black hair that had been turned into a riot of gypsy curls from constant sweating under the sun. His face was cooked to a leathery tan.

"What happened?" Revere asked. He was stunned. The man's presence was enough to bring him down from his coke high.

"I told you. They didn't get near the chick. Melonie had a fucking army this time. Wasted everybody. They only lost one man themselves."

"I see *you* made it back."

Deacon Archer shrugged. "Hey, man, I set it up. That's all. I wasn't about to die with that pack of pussies."

Revere fought to keep his control. Every minute that Melonie lived was a threat to him. He remembered all the publicity about her memoirs. *He* might show up there. Or a copy of the film with him in it might turn up in someone else's collection. Word of the Melonie Grand reissue series had everybody digging in their porno vaults. Anything to do with her meant money.

"We've got to silence her and everyone else on the list," Revere said. "Damn! We've got to hit her again. Use more deacons. I don't know what's wrong—you train them enough."

"Shit," Archer said. "It's not the training. It's the beast inside, man. You need the right man to begin with. Let me pick my own crew."

Revere shook his head. "I'm working with too many outsiders as it is. I want true believers *man enough* to die for the cause."

"The fuck with dying, man. Give me the word, and it'll get done right."

Revere swore. He scraped together another line of coke. "I have to go," he said. "We'll talk later." He ingested the powder while Deacon Archer looked on in disgust. Archer didn't like people who used drugs. He didn't mind selling it. He just didn't like depending on people under the influence. It was one of his damn rules of survival that he was always talking about.

Deacon Archer had been a Marine drill instructor. A wise-ass recruit had attacked him from behind during pugil-stick training. Archer killed him with one stroke of the stick. It was a reflex action, another one of his rules—*hit back, then find out what was going on.* For that he was dishonorably discharged. The wise-ass came from a family of influence.

Archer rode with a biker gang for a few years, but left when the randomness of life on the road lost its attraction. He set out on his own and flirted with the straight life. It wouldn't have him. He ended up serving time for robbery and murder. He was released on parole for a year before he was arrested on assault charges. Archer was scheduled to go back inside as a habitual felon when he saw the light and found religion. He was released in the custody of Luke Revere, who promised to watch over him and guide him.

The path led to the death of Melonie Grand.

Six

The three ICE agents filed into the penthouse apartment connected to Dartanian's office. They were freshly showered but still tired. A workout in the ninth floor gym didn't fade that easily.

Dartanian and Porter wore blocking bruises on their forearms and calves, courtesy of Sin Simara. The Japanese martial artist hardly pulled his punches or kicks when he trained with men of their caliber.

Though he wore the mask of a man who'd just come from a Saturday morning picnic, Simara had his share of black and blue marks. Porter's strength bulled him through Simara's defenses on occasion. Dartanian had tremendous speed and a daring that Simara rarely encountered.

Instead of blocking a kick, Dartanian often let it hit full force. This surprised his opponent for the crucial megasecond in which Dartanian retaliated twice as hard. Only a man hard enough to weather brutal punishment could pull it off. It was a matter of conditioning the body and the most important muscle of karate—the mind.

Dartanian grabbed two bottles of German beer for himself and Porter and a can of celery juice for

Simara. They sat on a horseshoe-shaped leather sofa and kicked up their feet on a round glass table. This was the site of informal think-tank sessions when they were on a case. It was two in the morning. The three of them had been working around the clock to zero in on the porn killers. One hot summer week had passed since the 49th Street assault, and they were nowhere near the man who called the shots. The workout had provided a needed release.

Mick raised his beer toward Simara. "To the day I knock you on your ass!"

"To your never-ending delusions." Simara toasted him with the small can of celery juice.

Dartanian sipped his beer and went to the window to look at the staggered city lights. Half of the city was dark and sleeping; the other half was working or prowling. This hour was quieter than usual. All the noises of the city had blended into a steady hum like the buzz of a giant transformer that powered New Yorkers for their manic race for survival. It was the sound of a living thing, an entity that demanded sacrifice.

He thought of the tabloids that called for his head after DSS liquidated the lunatics on 49th Street. Fortunately, Dartanian was able to defuse an explosive situation with the Midtown North precinct by calling on Alan Wise. Wise supervised a CIA domestic-operations group in the DSS building. He had enough pull to kill a special police investigation into Dartanian's activities.

"That turkey shoot of yours hit the national media," Wise had told him. "To put a lid on it, I used up my favors with three—count them—three top cops. But I damn near got you a presidential seal of approval."

"Every little bit helps," Dartanian had said.

Wise groaned. "Just remember who your friends are."

"You won't let me forget," Dartanian said. "But thanks. Call me when you need me."

Dartanian left the window to join his friends. He lit a Pall Mall and waited until his beer was finished before turning the conversation to business. "Let's get back to making the world safe for pornography," he said. He reviewed the case, starting with the six dead men who came after Melonie Grand.

The three men blown through the roof of the Chevy were untraceable. Of the other three, two were straights totally wrong for hit-man types. The last man was a loser who bounced around New York as a car-lot gofer, a dishwasher in a Brooklyn diner, and a short-lived campus security guard.

What brought this strange brew together? Dartanian put the ICE computer on all three and unleashed a squad of DSS agents to dig up their pasts.

Ed Demaris, the stocky hit man chopped down by Mick's Ingram, was an insurance agent from Wheeling, West Virginia. He moved to New York four years ago with a promotion to middle-level corporate management. His neighbors and coworkers had considered him a friendly man who got along well with everyone.

Robert Vandeveer, the thin man who was drastically out of place in the attack, was an accountant with the same firm for twenty years. His work record was meticulous bordering on obsession. He'd never missed a day of work. Outside the office, no one knew what made him click. He led a quiet life. His neighbors couldn't remember any conversations that went beyond the weather.

Larry Mott, who gunned down Craig Patroon, was a total write-off. After getting fired from a series of menial jobs, Mott was denied induction into the Marines, Army, and Air Force. The Army recruiter was shocked at the number of drugs Mott admitted abusing. The transcript showed that Mott said, "But everybody does those drugs, man. Don't they?"

An insurance man, an accountant, and a burnout. These were the men who made up half of a hit team. Only the insurance man had military training. He was a Korean vet. The other two were question marks. They obviously received some training for the attack, but where? What possessed them to come after Melonie Grand like a pack of demons?

Dartanian had found only one connection, and it was two years old and dying. Demaris and Vandeveer both had contributed significantly to the St. Theresa Foundation for the Elderly. The New York nonprofit institute donated medical equipment and nursing services to housebound senior citizens.

The foundation collapsed two years ago. Staff and records were abnormally difficult to trace. The bank accounts had vanished along with the personnel. Either it was a million-to-one coincidence that both hit men's tax records showed donations to the foundation and they subsequently turned into homicidal maniacs on their own—or the person behind the foundation brought them together for reasons of his own.

Dartanian covered the details quickly. Porter and Simara were ready to crash. Between guarding Melonie at the safe house and interrogating the porn figures she and Peter Cruz named, the ICE agents had little time for sleep.

They were forced to play a waiting game. The calm after the attack had lulled Melonie and Drew Wilson into a false security. Both thought all the killers were wiped out. The ICE men knew otherwise. Anyone capable of mounting such an attack wouldn't risk everything with one shot. Besides, the hitters were fanatics. They died for somebody. That somebody wasn't going to perish with them.

"Mick, you're to go all out on the foundation business. Any name that comes up, pounce on it. Even if they swear they never heard of St. Theresa, wear them down. Drive them crazy. Make a pest of yourself."

"In other words," Simara said. "Stay as you are."

Dartanian turned to Simara. "You can visit our good friend Drew Wilson. Scare some sense into him. Tell him if he doesn't come around, I'm cutting him loose."

Dartanian threw an occasional tail on Wilson on the slim chance he might lead them down some underground avenues worth walking. Melonie's manager was secretive and uncooperative about the irons he had in the porn fire. He thought he was playing Dartanian for a fool by keeping him in the dark.

"What's he doing?" Simara asked.

"It's what he's not doing. He's not consulting me before talking to the press. And he's keeping a high profile. The man is one visible asshole. He thinks the killers are gone because he wants them to be gone."

For once in his life, Drew Wilson was a media figure. Gossip columnists courted him nightly because he was an insider. The *Post* ran an item about Wilson's security tactics that nailed the hit team. Other dailies ran features on the "genius" behind *Starlet* and his future film projects.

"Okay," Simara said. "I'll handle Wilson. Mick checks out the foundation." He smiled and asked a question he already knew the answer to. "What dragon will you slay?"

Dartanian sighed and then grinned. "I'm afraid that leaves me with Melonie. I'll concentrate on her."

"We've all been concentrating on her," Simara said. "*Damn,* this business gets rough at times."

Dartanian met with Peter Cruz the next day. The porn director had set up a temporary studio in a luxury hotel on Central Park South. He'd been patching up *Starlet* ever since Dartanian postponed shooting on the film.

The dapper director hunched over a Steenbeck editing console, while Dartanian questioned him. Periodically, he froze a scene from *Starlet*. Cruz viewed the most explicit sex footage with the same eye he used on a cup of coffee. Years of exposure killed any erotic thrill from porn. He was a technician doing his job.

"I visited every contact you gave me," Dartanian said. He'd talked to veteran porn actresses, stage actors doing sex films on the side, models who did one film just to get discovered, and every breed of hustler in-between.

"Learn anything?" Cruz asked.

"Nothing useful," Dartanian said. "It was like talking to Martians."

Cruz laughed. "You're lucky I just deal with the cream of the crop. There's others in this business that can turn your hair white in an hour."

Dartanian waited for an explanation, while Cruz worked the editing console.

"It's like the old saying 'Lie down with dogs, get up with pups,' " Cruz said. "There are chicks out there who will hump animal, vegetable, or mineral for 20 bucks. Let's be happy I don't know any of them personally."

"It's a deal," Dartanian said. The human wreckage he'd already encountered in the porn world left vivid memories. What were they like on the next lower rung of the ladder?

Cruz shut off the Steenbeck machine and bummed a smoke from Dartanian. Despite the outward calm, Cruz had nervous eyes. He didn't relish working on a project that someone had chosen as a target. "So where are we?" the director demanded. "I mean, is someone gonna blow my head off when I leave the hotel, or is it just my basic paranoia acting up? I mean, Melonie's putting out that it's over, man."

"Melonie thinks a lot of crazy things," Dartanian said. He joined Cruz in a smoke. They walked to the sitting room where a floor-to-ceiling window viewed Central Park. "Take my advice. Keep up the precautions I showed you. Something out there likes to hit hard. It's coming back."

"Why?" Cruz asked.

"I'm asking you," Dartanian said. He went over the script again to see if there was any scene that might trigger an attack from someone. And he probed Cruz for any possible enemies. After all, it was a rough business.

"I've done what you said," Cruz responded. "I tried to think of guys out to waste me or the cast. Drew a blank. Hey, compared to some sharks in this racket, I'm an immensely likable guy. You can ask everybody, man."

Dartanian nodded. "I did."

Cruz inhaled a half inch of cigarette. He exhaled a smoky sigh and threw up his hands, "Fuck, it could be anything. It could be a looney tune wanting his name in the papers."

"Maybe it's in the flick itself," Dartanian said. "I notice your script plays with the theory that Marilyn Monroe was assassinated. Maybe someone wants to make art imitate life."

"Nah. The Marilyn Monroe hit? Hey, there's a lot of stories about her getting wasted for banging the wrong boy, but we just dance around it. We hardly touch it in *Starlet*."

"You and I know that," Dartanian pointed out. "But suppose she was hit. Suppose the killers think you're pointing a finger at them. They want the flick stopped at any case."

Cruz reached for another cigarette. "That's a bit outlandish, ain't it"

"Nothing's outlandish these days."

Sin Simara skipped up the half flight of stairs tacked onto the fifth floor of the Nordic Apartments as an afterthought. The building housed students from nearby New York University and a few odd souls like Drew Wilson.

A bronze plaque on the door read *Drew Wilson Theatrical Company*. Must be his idea of a low profile, Simara thought. Despite Dartanian's suggestion to move out until the killers were found, Wilson stayed on in his den. He couldn't bear to leave the fresh supply of actresses. His best recruits came from college students. It was amazing how many of the bright young things worked porn to fund their education.

The Japanese man turned the knob when no one responded to his knock. He twisted his wrist and popped the lock. Simara pushed the door inward. Lazy jazz music floated from a back room. "Hello!" he shouted. Still no answer. He stepped over throw pillows scattered in the living room.

Simara thought he might be too late. Perhaps one of the assassins got Wilson and left the music playing loud to cover his passing. He walked slowly down the hallway. Shades were drawn to keep the apartment dim. Simara doubted the killer would still be here, but he never took chances. He had to act as if a killer waited for him. Simara couldn't surprise him, not after shouting like a yahoo.

The apartment bore a scent of death.

Simara eased into two connecting bedrooms. One served as a storeroom. The other was the world-famous office of the Drew Wilson Theatrical Company. A rolltop desk was covered with a mass of papers, photographs, and videotapes. Two cluttered hardback chairs flanked the desk. Simara froze when he heard a sound from the last room on the left.

He approached on silent feet, crept to the open door, and burst into the room. A woman gasped. She was naked and writhing on top of Drew Wilson. No more than 20, the brunette's eyes freaked at Simara's entrance.

"What's a nice girl like you doing on a face like this?" Simara asked.

Drew Wilson sputtered and threw the girl off. "Get out of here!" he yelled. The scrawny hustler glared at Simara. "What the hell is this?"

His startled companion leaned forward to dip

her breasts into a frilly red bra. "You *promised* me a part," she whined.

"Take a walk, tramp," Wilson said.

She slapped his face. He swung back. Simara broke up their girlish duel. He lifted her so only one foot touched the floor. He twisted Wilson's wrist until he knelt.

"Mr. Wilson will keep his promises," Simara said. "Right?"

"Yesss!" Wilson hissed. "Let me go. Owww! You got a part in my next flick."

She winked at Simara, bundled her skirt and sandals, and skipped out of the bedroom. Simara released his grip.

The ax-faced man fell onto the bed and nursed his tortured wrist. He looked ridiculous with his stork legs sticking out of bright red briefs. "You can't barge in here like some Gestapo creep!" Wilson said.

"The facts speak otherwise," Simara corrected him. "Actually, I was just demonstrating the weakness of your security."

"Spare me the bullshit, Confucius. Let's get this over with. What do you want this time?"

"Like I said, I came here to warn you."

"Oh, man, don't start with that *danger* crap. That Dartanian cat's in it for the money. Naturally, he wants us to think we're in danger. He can rip off some more bucks from the Taplin people that way."

Simara's eyes went cold. He speared the soft underside of Wilson's chin with a rigid index finger. The man grunted and craned his head back. "I can't change your mind," Simara said. "But I *can* change your face. Show some respect."

Wilson nodded. He grabbed an expensive robe

from the foot of the bed and draped it over his shoulders. Even with the flashy threads, he still looked like a derelict from the Bowery. It was that special quality in his weasel eyes.

Simara recited his sins. Wilson had been seen purchasing film videotapes from several sources without reporting it. His deal with Taplin involved buying old movies of Melonie for reissue as a Classic Film. His deal with Dartanian called for duplicates of all films and information on the people who sold them.

"How do you know all that?"

Simara smiled. "You've been followed. Just like *Candid Camera*. You're the star, fella."

"Then you know who sold me the films."

"Sure. But *you* tell us anyway. We want cooperation."

Wilson rattled off several names including his best supplier, Ralph Hendricks. Hendricks was supposed to sell another batch of Melonie material, but he missed his appointment with Wilson.

"Where can I find him?" Simara asked.

"Hey, man, he dropped out of sight."

Simara mimicked him. "*He dropped out of sight.* You're supposed to tell us anything suspicious, and you let that go by."

"Nothing suspicious," Wilson said. "This is porn, baby. People come and go all the time. Get me?"

"I'm afraid we're stuck with you," Simara said.

Seven

Deacon Archer cut the blue Harley's engine and whispered into the alley. The street crawled with night people in search of easy money. After ten o'clock, the neighborhood was rough. That didn't matter to Archer. He dismounted from the chopper and grabbed a small leather case from the baggage rack.

Two men blocked the mouth of the alley. They'd come to check him out. The black man had a white sleeveless T-shirt and loose khaki pants. He was short, but he was obviously a weight lifter, with muscles jumping on top of each other. A legionnaire's cap shadowed his eyes. The white hood was taller and just as solid. Greasy brown hair fell down to his shoulders.

Archer recognized the breed. They were young and nowhere, strictly disposable. He closed the gap between them like they weren't there.

"This is our alley, man," the white one said. He stepped forward to shake a finger at Archer. "What the fuck are *you* doing here?"

Archer deflected the pointing hand and grabbed him by the throat. "Whatever I want," he said. He plastered the young tough against the brick wall.

His left palm stiff-armed the air between him and the black as a warning. The discount legionnaire didn't move. "Any more questions?" Archer asked. A hard squeeze made the brick-sniffing hood spit out the pain.

The eyes bulged from his contorted face, but he managed to shake his head no.

Archer smiled "Since we get along so well, I'm putting you in charge of my bike." He jerked his head toward the back of the alley. "If anything's wrong when I come back, I'm gonna bash your brains to gravy. Don't think I won't chase your ass down if I have to. I got all the time in the world."

His long hair swayed up and down. Archer gave him back his throat with a shove to the front of the alley. He gasped and coughed and acted like he really was Archer's friend. His head couldn't nod enough. "We'll take care of it, man," he said. "No sweat, right?"

"Shit," said the black. "Piece a cake."

Archer pushed through the two men. He hadn't wanted a scene, but he didn't want to come back to a stripped down Harley either. As he walked away he heard the legionnaire say, "You showed *his* ass to the door, brother."

Luke Revere's head deacon pushed them out of his mind. They weren't the type to remember him if the cops came around. Besides, his business was four blocks away, and that was a whole other world.

Deacon Archer covered the ground fast. He walked two blocks, then cut through Washington Square where drug dealers and burn artists assaulted anyone who came by—except Deacon Archer. He was looking mean, unlike the way he first acted in the alley. The highwaymen worked in packs to hound the gamblers who risked a walk through the park. They demanded money for drugs, oregano, or safe passage.

Archer strolled past New York University, then slowed to a casual walk as he neared his target. He entered a neglected apartment building between two well-kept brownstones. Archer took the stairs two at a time without raising a sweat. He pounded the hell out of a door with a plaque that read Drew Wilson Theatrical Company.

There was no response.

"Wilson!" he shouted. He thumped it harder. A moment later the door opened two inches. Drew Wilson peered cautiously through the space. A shiny new chain lock held the door in place.

"What is it?"

"You Drew Wilson?"

"Who wants to know?"

Deacon Archer glared at him. He recognized the face that appeared so often on television bragging of his behind-the-scenes work with the *Starlet* ensemble.

"Yes," Wilson said, unable to meet the fierce gaze. "I'm Wilson." He tried to push the door shut without being obvious. His slow pressure gradually built to a constant shove.

It was a useless move. Archer's hand had flattened out on the door the moment Wilson opened it. It was a reflex. He easily neutralized Wilson.

"What do you want?" the thin-faced man asked.

He waved the leather case in his left hand. "It's what you want, if you're the guy paying for Melonie films."

"How'd you find me?"

"A guy named Hendricks turned me on to you. He wanted to buy 'em from me but, hell, I figured why deal with a middleman so I come straight to you."

Drew nodded his head. The man talked his language. "So whadda ya got?"

"Three films of Melonie in the raw that'll stiffen a bishop. Come on, is you the man or is you ain't?" Archer stomped his feet and half turned. "Don't waste my time."

"Hold on." Wilson inched the door closed and unhooked the chain.

Deacon Archer stepped inside and looked at the shapeless pillow furniture. "What happened? Your parachute crash?"

"What?"

"Get me something to sit on."

Wilson went to the kitchen for a chair. The big man followed him and looked in every room they passed. He picked up a hardbacked chair and brought it to the living room where he straddled it backwards.

Drew Wilson perched on his sofa like a parakeet about to get fed. "Let's see the goods."

"Sure," Archer said. He unzipped the small leather case, digging the look of anticipation on Wilson's face.

"Oh, shit," Wilson said when the hand came out.

"Uh-huh," Archer responded. He waved a 9mm Heckler & Koch VP70 at the slight man. He seemed to shrink even more at the sight of the pistol.

"What are you here for?" Wilson asked. His voice was timid. If he talked low enough, maybe the man would go away.

"Let's talk," Archer said.

* * *

Peggy Revere, the all-American wife, looked great in anything but she looked especially great in the wig. It added a hint of wickedness to her soft, tanned face. The wig was long and black with rows of curls. She resembled a country-and-western singer down on her luck, riding on nothing but her looks and a tremendous chest.

"I'm looking for work," she told the manager of the Esteem Health Spa and Oriental Massage Parlor. "Any kind of work."

"I believe it," he said. He inspected the well-filled silver blouse. Lasso-shaped seams circled the bodice. Half of the pearl snap buttons were undone. He and a trashy redhead sat at a table behind the cash register counter. The redhead shook her head when he left to get a close-up look at Peggy.

His name was Lester Pratt. He was fiftyish and wore a gold medallion on his gray-haired chest. Like Peggy, his shirt was half open but the effect was nowhere near as enticing. Lester leaned on the counter with a *Look what I found* grin on his face. "What kind of experience ya got?"

"Anything worth having."

"Ahhh, we got a real live one here!" He turned to wink at the redhead. She changed her icy expression to a friendly smile until he turned back to Peggy.

Peggy mentioned the ad in the *Village Voice* for trained masseuses. Lester gave her a one-minute con about the Esteem being a clean operation. "None of that sex stuff here."

The redhead choked back a laugh.

Lester raised his eyebrow at her and continued his rap. According to Lester, a man who spent nearly 20 years as a porn actor, the girls in his place were different from the kind who worked the live-sex show, escort service, and parlor girl circuit. To tell the truth, most of them were fresh out of the convent.

"This is a health establishment," he said, ending his spiel.

"Let's get healthy," she said.

He smiled. She passed the initial screening. Lester turned on the charm and grabbed the fleshy swell of her ass as he guided her behind the counter. He fancied himself the Hugh Hefner of the East Coast, although he never would be anything more than the Lester Pratt of the Aging Porn Actor's Guild. No one had noticed when he retired from the business.

"Take over for me," he said to the redhead.

"Of course, Mr. Pratt," she squeaked in her best impression of an executive secretary. She took a hard look at Peggy as she passed. The heavily made-up secretary appeared to be analyzing her as if she couldn't understand why her boss was so hot for the newcomer's body.

Peggy couldn't tell if she was overdressed, underdressed, or simply had too much class to fit in with the Esteem girls. *Jealous . . . the girl was jealous of her.* Why be jealous over a wreck like Pratt?

The back office had white paneling and roach-colored wall-to-wall carpeting. Past glories of Lester Pratt's life hung on the walls. Where doctor's displayed their credentials above their desks, Pratt had a dozen photos of half-naked women clinging to him. Some of the shots were from his flicks. Others were amateur snapshots.

More photos stood on the corners of his desk, a massive wooden square that had been here for a hundred years or more. Instead of family portraits, Lester had X-rated snapshots of a blond girl instantly recognizable.

"Is that you and . . ."

"Melonie Grand," he bragged. "Me and her go back a long time. We still keep in touch, though it's hard to see each other. Both of us have pretty tight schedules. You know we almost got married?"

Lester came around his desk and stepped behind Peggy. His hands skidded down the peaks of her silvery blouse and settled on her stomach.

Peggy pried loose. She was in charge now. She sashayed over to a blue sofa bed and kicked off her heels.

Lester sat on the edge of his desk. The gold medallion slapped against his chest like a porn flake's dog tag. So many people in the business wore them that it seemed to be part of a uniform. "You know, a lot of girls come in here and say they balled King Kong, but they freeze when it's put up time. It's my job to make sure you're not like that. See what I'm saying?"

She snapped open her blouse to answer.

"Right," he said. He turned up the volume on his desk radio.

Peggy stood and unwrapped the skirt. It fell on top of her high heels. She shook her head and pushed back the ridiculous long curls of the wig to keep them out of her bra.

"Nice," Lester said. "But cops go this far sometimes for entrapment. You have to initiate everything. Understand?"

"Ummm-hmmmn," she said. She slid to the floor and knelt over the couch with the cushion scraping her soft belly. Her stockings caught on the rough carpeting. "How's this for understanding?"

she said, rolling her satin panties down to her knees.

He laughed. "Just so we understand each other." He took her from behind a moment later. She gasped. There was no time for preparation. It was just like one of his damn movies. She shuddered with each push inside. This was a first for her. He'd done it so many times in the movies that it was second nature.

Peggy played her part to the hilt. She sighed and grunted and pounded back on him. But the scenario she acted out was created by Luke Revere. The final act was yet to come. She postponed her pleasure until then.

Lester climbed off and collapsed onto the floor. He lit a cigarette and leaned back onto the sofa. He was drained of life for a short time.

"Now it's my turn, lover," she said. She reached inside her large carry all purse.

"Huh?"

He turned and looked into the barrel of a silenced KG9. "Mmmmmmmn," Peggy moaned and squeezed the trigger. She popped the 32-round clip of 9mm slugs into his head in three seconds. The thwacking sound of the bullets was just like the melons Deacon Archer had her practice on.

She sat on the sofa and prodded her bra cups with the smoking gun. At one time, it had been a legal pistol. Deacon Archer fixed that with a cutting tool and 30 seconds of his time. Now it was a machine pistol. "This is your friend and lover from now on," Deacon had told the inner circle of deacons when he handed them out. Peggy Revere was the only one to take him literally. Two minutes later, she got up from the couch, dressed, and left the room.

"He wants to see you, sweetheart," she said to the redhead in the outer office.

"Why'nt the fuck he tell me hisself?" she said. She walked into the room of loud music. Peggy Revere stepped in behind her and closed the door.

Before the redhead had a chance to scream, Peggy whacked her with another clip. The redhead danced across the room, stitched from heel to head. She tumbled over the mess that used to be Lester Pratt.

"Such a nice couple," Peggy said. She closed the door to give them some privacy.

That night, Avery Fischer Hall flooded Broadway with waves of concertgoers. Among the well-heeled crowd discussing the performance of the New York Philharmonic was Harold Freed. He had a black tux, sported a cane, and waxed his hair down the middle like a gentleman from another era. His movie-matinee face was familiar to porn audiences for the last decade.

Beneath the elegant costume lived a world-class hedonist. He was seen around town with an ongoing series of legitimate actresses who fell under him like a row of dominoes. Word passed from one actress to the next that Harold Freed was a "must." He was acceptable in high society. Educated and charming, Freed was a badge to be worn by the "in" crowd. The actresses didn't find out how depraved he was until they experienced him firsthand. He provided them all with a wicked initiation into a private club. They were too embarrassed afterward to admit what hoops he forced them through. Consequntly, the legend of his charm and technique spread like a social disease.

"There he is," Peggy Revere said. "Pull over. Now, dammit! He's getting away."

The white Rolls Royce joined the herd of limos waiting to pick up the Philharmonic crowd. Peggy hopped out of the Rolls and strolled down the street. She wore a white evening dress cut low enough for a string of pearls to dip in and out of her cleavage. She was in her favorite role tonight—the southern belle showing enough décolletage to snare any gentleman.

She bumped into Harold Freed from behind. "Oh, I'm so terribly sorry," she apologized. Peggy clutched his arms as she tumbled forward. Her breasts mashed against him. "I'm *sooooo* clumsy." Her voice dripped with southern honey.

Freed coolly studied her. After a while, he blessed her with a Greek god smile.

"Aren't you—I can't believe my luck—aren't you Harold Freed?"

"Yes. You know me from my work?"

She faked a blush. "Well, I guess we do share the same interests. There's the, uh, concerts, and uh, there's your work."

Freed smiled for real. This wasn't the first time he'd been recognized by a society dame. Nor was it the first time one of them forced an introduction on him in such a clumsy manner. They were usually the best kind, however, since they were so eager to please.

"Your films fascinate me," she said. "Imagine! Meeting Harold Freed in person! I wish I could talk to you some more."

"Sure it's the films that fascinate you?" He considered her a typical rich bitch dripping with jewelry and a lust for kicks. It was the statistic that attracted her kind. Harold "12½" Freed was a freak to some, a god to others. This air-head southern bitch was definitely a worshiper, he thought.

"Let me take you to dinner," she said.

"When?"

"Right now. I'm very *hungry*."

"Subtle, too." He showed his teeth. "I suppose that next you're going to tell me you're looking for a taste of the fast life."

She grabbed his arm. "My car's over there."

Harold saw the Rolls and immediately made up his mind. He let her lead him to the Rolls like a trophy bagged in the wilds. He leaned into the soft back seat cushion, then, startled, he ran his hand over the smooth surface. "Tacky," he said. The white leather was wrapped tight with a plastic cover.

"Take us around Central Park," Peggy said.

The driver nodded and swung into traffic. Freed paid no attention to him or to the scenery. He made himself at home in the plush traveling bedroom. Freed sighed. He acted passive, almost bored, while she administered to him.

She opened her mouth to breathe on his neck before kissing. The teasing action made him laugh. "Don't bother," he said. Peggy kissed him. Her lips were like the fangs of a black widow spider searching for a weak spot on the well-toned body. Freed was statuesque, an elegant product for an elegant consumer.

"Get down to business," he said. "I don't have time for fooling around." He exposed himself and thought she overdid it when she gasped. She stared at his long inert member with fear and awe. It was just what she wanted, though. This one was no different from the rest of the pack.

"Feast on it with more than your eyes, huh?" He guided her head. Freed took a long time.

Peggy came up for air, wiped her wet mouth,

and reached into her purse. She moved across from him and leaned on the other window while she applied a tube of lipstick. "I'm finished," she said to the driver.

Another discreet chauffeur, Harold thought. Another bored rich bitch. The porn star barely looked at the driver. Like all servants, they were best when they were invisible.

The driver stopped the car, turned, and quickly became visible. The pistol in his hand helped. Suddenly, Freed knew what the plastic cover was for. The bitch didn't want to get the Rolls messy.

Deacon Archer fired once. The 9mm slug from the VP 70 whipped Freed's head to the right. It looked like he shook his head no in a violent argument. It was his last.

"Nice shot," Peggy coohed.

"Fuck you," Archer said..

Harold Freed's last role was a corpse in a makeshift body bag tossed along a deserted stretch of the Hudson. After he dumped the body, Deacon Archer settled down for the ride up to White Plains. He didn't say a word to Peggy Revere. He hated the cold-hearted whore. She *had* to have her fun with the man before Deacon wasted him.

He went along with it only because Peggy Revere, little Miss America, was a dangerous broad to cross. She got what she wanted, or else she was murder. Archer didn't put it past her to convince Luke Revere that Archer was dispensable.

They were both cut from the same bad cloth. Luke and his lovable wife killed because it satisfied a need inside of them. Archer killed because it was his business. Now they were all partners in a carnival of sin masquerading as Luke Revere's Ministry of the Air.

It had been good in the beginning. Archer worked as a bodyguard for Revere, then as his bag man for all of the political contributions. When he moved up into the blackmail scams and the occasional hits, he was rewarded beyond his dreams.

Then things got out of hand. It was no longer a matter of wasting someone who stood in Revere's way. Now it was an all-out war. Revere's crazy list grew longer every day, despite the number of dead. He locked himself in his chapel with treasure troves of pornography films and videotapes. Any connection at all that he found between Melonie Grand and an actor was a death warrant.

Archer remembered all of the jaunts Revere took into the city to haunt the porno stores, to ferret out the names of the stars who shared Melonie's bed, and therefore—in Revere's mind—her secrets.

The hit list was their twisted version of the Bible. Peggy and Luke spent hours planning the deaths, enlisting Deacon Archer in their councils. Often they had the porn tapes running in the background to stir them up and get the creative juices flowing.

At times, Peggy came on to Archer, wanting to have a three-way with Luke. But he drew the line there. She was poison. He'd made it with her when Luke first signed her up on the team. But then he found out what a death-loving bitch she was.

Peggy Archer had a dozen scalps on her garter belt long before Revere "saved" her. She worked with a three-man gang who bashed the little sense out of suckers Peggy lured from a bar to the alley where they waited. Conventioneers or just plain drunks would follow her once she teased them to fever pitch.

Instead of the promised quickie, they got a fucking-over that took years of recovery. She'd open their shirts, unzip their pants, and step aside while the three goons stomped the man.

One of Peggy's suckers died and was traced to the gang. There had been other corpses before, but the police attributed them to random violence. This murder led right to her door. The press made a big deal of the case. They plastered her bar-girl image all over the papers and called her a sultry victim of circumstance.

Revere's weakness for whores prompted him to pay her bail anonymously. He followed that with a high-priced lawyer who pulled a Pygmalion act on her. The lawyer toned down her hard-ass nature and taught her how to act like the "girl next door." The jury bought her claim that she was an innocent girl forced to act under duress. She walked out of court a free bird.

Luke Revere swooped down on her and took her under his wing. Within a week, he had his hooks into her. He fell hard for the vicious beauty, but to be on the safe side he taped her private confessions. In case she ever turned on him, he had a sword to bring down on her pretty neck.

It was a match made in hell, and Deacon Archer found himself right in the middle. The two sickos believed they were invincible. Their murders grew more daring. Archer suspected they no longer were capable of seeing the backlash that was bound to come from their terror reign. Their bloodlust pumped up the hit list with every passing day. Now that they'd started, they never wanted the slaughter to end.

Revere used comprehensive dossiers and personal interviews with Ministry members to pick out the fanatics ripe for training. He had a knack for sensing the right type of nut. Some had military training. Others were rank amateurs. But all of them had the death wish of the true zealot.

The charismatic preacher was a modern Mohammed who instinctively grasped the military use of fanatics. Whereas Mohammed had promised glory and wealth in heaven if they died in battle, Luke Revere gave his followers a taste of heaven on earth. Aside from the lavish quarters for his deacons, Revere supplied them with wealth, women, and indoctrination—all in the name of God.

Once the deacons were selected, it was Archer's task to train them. Archer got the weapons. He taught them basic warfare tactics. Although they learned the essentials, the problem with the deacons was their pack mentality. They weren't too good when it came to thinking for themselves.

Archer wanted to form his own private army of real fighters like himself. Until then, he was stuck with these good Christian soldiers. The deacons were ready to battle Satan's legions—as soon as Revere put them on the list.

Eight

PORN STARS BLOWN AWAY. The *Post* headline would have been laughable any other time, but Melonie's humor was choked by the knowledge that the assassins were still at large. This latest round of killings was just a teaser. Melonie was the main feature. She tossed the paper to the bedroom floor.

The safe house had become a pampered cell for Melonie Grand. Every comfort but freedom was hers for the asking. Like other prisoners, she turned to keeping a diary. At Dartanian's urging, she tried to reconstruct her calendar for the past decade. Every day she jotted down the details as they came to her. She had compiled a foot-high stack of notebooks of scorching memoirs. If nothing else, she was finally churning out the much-touted autobiography she'd contracted for. Actually, it was Drew Wilson who contracted for it. He sold the project, and she went along with it. That was the pattern of her life. She went along.

Men had decided her life. Now they would decide her death—unless she discovered what past sin demanded such killing punishment.

Drew Wilson was shot to death in his apartment. Harold Freed turned up in a blood-stained plastic baggie along the Hudson River. Lester Pratt and a parlor girl were splattered all over his office. The tabloids screamed murder all the way to the bank.

Melonie's lack of feeling for Drew Wilson surprised Melonie herself. Her manager was dead. So what? She needed a new manager. The only grief she felt was a shaky tremor in her soul because the killers were getting closer to her. They had fewer outside targets to blast.

Wilson had been a pain in the ass, and that's what had made him such a good manager. Friends who told her to get rid of him long ago didn't understand that his reputation as a vulture was responsible for squeezing out that extra percentage. Everyone knew that he was a hard bargainer.

She threaded another film in the projector. Stacks of 8mm films and videotapes bordered all sides of the bed. The collection grew each day. Dartanian's agents hit the porn stores in the New York area in search of any film that carried her likeness. In the early days of porn, the producers and stars weren't too keen on having their names listed. Porn didn't become fashionable and quasi legal until she served five years of hard time in front of the kleig lights.

As a result, Melonie viewed hundreds of films that turned out to feature an actress that resembled her. Sometimes she found herself spliced in at the end of a reel containing performers she'd never seen before. After the first half hour of viewing, she felt like novocaine coursed through her thighs. Her eyes turned waxen. It was worse than watching television, but she had to do it. One of those X-rated interludes might trigger the right memory.

Some time in her past, she'd slept with a killer. Unless she found him out, he was going to put her to bed for keeps.

Dartanian found her sleeping on the carpet, with her head resting on clasped hands. A blank screen lit the room in front of her prone form. A played-out reel of film flapped on the projector.

He looked down at her and smiled. Production on *Starlet* was postponed, yet she still made herself up as Marilyn Monroe every day. She wore tight black hip-huggers and a zebra-striped midriff. Her fluffy blond hair slightly covered her eyes.

"Melonie." He spoke softly, then rapped his knuckles on the door.

She stirred.

"Melonie, it's me. Dartanian."

"Mmmmmn," purred her sleepy lips. Melonie stretched and smiled. Her eyes fluttered wide open. She saw the tall man standing over her and snapped up in a sitting position. Her right hand grasped the shag rug. She was ready to flee when her mind caught up to her startled eyes. "Oh, God, it's you! I thought for a second someone broke in."

"No one gets this far unless we want him to. You should know that by now."

She nodded and hugged her knees. "You said we would try something new tonight." She pursed her glossy red lips and batted her lashes. "Does that mean you're not made of ice after all?"

Close, he thought. He stepped over her bare feet and riffled through the newest pages of loose leaf notes. "We'll try something new. But first we'll go over the same old questions."

Melonie got to her feet and brushed the back of her slacks. She turned to Dartanian and asked if she'd got all of the dust off. He shook his head. She always came on to him like this. If she wasn't calling attention to her ass or chest, she was wetting her lips and winking at him. She wanted Marilyn Monroe to live just as much as someone else wanted her to die a second death.

"How well did you know Lester Pratt?"

"Not very. I did a troupe bit with him. A dozen of us hung out for a week at this guy's mansion. We banged out about twenty loops altogether. One night, after he has a bondage scene with me, he asked me to marry him. Haven't seen the goof since."

"Harold Freed ring any bells?" Dartanian asked.

"Not mine," she leered. "But I did three feature films with him. We were a hot number to the public, but it went no further. He was a genuine creep."

Dartanian edged aside a pile of papers and sat on the desk. After pacing the room and doing a few yoga stretches, Melonie took her customary position on the bed. She kept both hands flat on the mattress and kicked her heels over the side. She looked down at the floor, while her feet tapped against the sideboard. She reminded him of a child sitting on a dock looking down into the water, fishing for memories.

No matter how blasé she claimed to be, Melonie rarely met his eyes when he questioned her. It wasn't caused by anything on his part. Dartanian had warred too long to be shocked by human or inhuman deeds. Her moral lapses seemed trivial compared to the world's pain. No, he thought. The reason for her faltering gaze under questioning was a conscience crying to be heard.

"Whatever the relationships were," Dartanian

said, "we're interested in what they appear to be. On film at least, you were repeatedly involved with both men. That's enough to make someone think you could be connected off screen."

"Who knows what porn fans think?" she said. "They're all scary to me."

"Maybe you're scary to them."

"What do you mean?"

"You're the perfect woman, Melonie. On screen, you become a goddess. And what man can measure up to that image?"

"I keep looking," she snapped.

"I'm saying that you might be such a threat to someone that he has to remove you from the set. Whoever he is, he's got some strange allies."

"One of them is still in my dreams, the sonofabitch! I hope to God he was in the car you blasted." A mixture of anger and helplessness reddened her pretty face. The emotions neutralized one another and left her sitting there with no way to spend her energy.

"Even if he *was* killed," Dartanian said, "there are a lot more involved. We have to find out what the hell brings an accountant, an insurance man, and God knows what else to the point of murder. We've got to find out now."

"I guess I'm just the kiss of death," she said. She gave him a *poor girl in trouble* look meant to pull a denial out of him.

"You got it," Dartanian said. He lit one of his Pall Malls. Melonie tapped one out of the pack and stuck it in her mouth. She lit hers by pressing against the one in his lips. Anything to get close, he thought. Anything to wear down his defenses. She sure as hell had the right kind of weapons. Dartanian gripped her shoulders, turned her around, and marched her back to the bed.

She flopped onto the bed and rested against the headboard. Dartanian discussed the murders since the beginning of the case and then probed her memory, setting her up for what was to follow. "The reasoning behind the attacks is most likely the killer's assumption that you shared some explosive info with the men in your life, the close ones."

"I've never been attached to any man." She blew a smoke ring toward the ceiling. "Until now."

Dartanian probed her memory one more time. He took her back to year one for a quick refresher and then brought her back to the present. When he told her what the next phase was, Melonie acted shocked.

"Oh, really?" she said, jumping into her breathless Monroe persona. "What do you know about hypnosis?"

He smiled. The MKULTRA and ARTICHOKE projects came to mind, along with several other CIA programs that tested hypnosis and drugs for interrogation and brainwashing purposes. Dartanian had practiced hypnosis on his field agents in Nam to turn off the stress that made so many of them burn out. He'd also taken part in a program where hypnosis was used to create alter egos for deep-cover agents who would actually become other personalities until they were activated.

"I know a little bit about the field," he said. "Enough to realize the average person is hypnotized without knowing it up to thirty times a day. Television, music, driving in your car, anything can do it. We just take it a step further."

"Why wait until now?" Melonie asked.

Dartanian explained that memory was selective and adjustable. The subject often altered or created memories to please the hypnotist, or operator. A person in a trance state was vulnerable to suggestion and wish fulfillment. The desire to nail an assailant could cause a subject to manufacture a false memory just because a suspect was available. There were other dangers of hypnosis. A person could become fixated on a certain area and ignore more important data. More times than not, the beliefs of the operator became the beliefs of the subject.

"That's why it was best to re-create a conscious account of the past ten years," Dartanian said. "We can use that as a control against any 'memories' that surface under hypnosis." He told her about the UFO cases he'd worked on where people who'd never seen UFOS fantasized memories under hypnosis. They were just as detailed as the reports given by genuine UFO witnesses under hypnosis. "Hypnosis is a wonderful tool, but it's far from exact," he continued. "Look at the thousands of people who've regressed to past lives under hypnosis and discovered they were all Cleopatra. Talk about multiple personalities!"

Melonie was interested. "It sounds kind of freaky. Imagine having Melonie Grand under your control. You realize how many guys would give their right nut to be in your shoes?"

"Three million," he said. "Give or take a few." He neglected to tell her another reason for waiting until now for hypnosis. Dartanian had expected Mick Porter's look into the St. Theresa Foundation to turn up leads long before this. That was the only connection between the dead assassins. It was time to grasp at every straw. Before setting up another trap where Melonie was the bait, Dartanian wanted to squeeze out every bit of information. If hypnosis didn't work, then he would try narcotherapy. The body count was rising fast. He got Melonie's permission to try both methods.

It didn't take long to put her under. She was willing, and her trance capacity was high. With the aid of her yoga exercises, Dartanian totally relaxed her while directing her in a soft chant. He brought her to the countdown state, itself a powerful suggestion. Since the subject fully expected to be put under at a certain point, the simple act of counting out loud, "Five . . . four . . . three . . . two . . . one . . ." served as a direct ladder to the unconscious state. From there it was a matter of regressing her to a specific point in the past. His voice stayed soft but authoritative. She followed his commands back to her college days. Then he played her like a reel of tape.

Dartanian felt like the ultimate eavesdropper as he weaved in and out of her sex life. She responded to him as though he were a confessor and here was her chance to get it all out. Melonie relived her past with panting, crying, shouting, and laughing. It was the first time she'd really been stripped naked in years. For once in her life, she shed more than her clothes.

The shell of sophistication cracked when she said, "I wish I could walk away, that it never started. Uhhh, it's disgusting, but I'll do it. I'll do anything. Gonna be a star." She opened to him but revealed no new information until he brought her back to her early college days for a second look.

"We're at your motel again. The party's turning into a group scene. You said before there were some strange people with you."

She giggled like a drunk. "They're all strange. Dopers, straights, bikers . . . even a *preacher.*" Her laugh shot up again at the mention of the preacher. "What a night!"

"How'd you feel that night?"

"Fucked up," she said. "We were all fucked up. And I was fucking with this guy's head. The preacher who wasn't a preacher."

"What was he?"

"Hmmmm?"

"The preacher. What was he?"

"Con man. He was a fucking con man, and you shoulda seen him talk. Silver-tongued boy preacher gone bad. I always wanted to bang a preacher. Mmmmmmn-hmmmmmmn. Said I was a confused child. *He* was the confused one. Straightened him out hard!"

"What's his name?"

She shook her head from left to right, then dropped into a form of dream paralysis that often gripped people in a trance state.

"Where did you meet him?"

She laid there silent as a corpse. Dartanian worked on her for several minutes until she spoke again. "Take me home," she said. "Bring me back. *Please!* Curt! Curt! He's got a gun. Oh God, he's shooting. Don't kill me!" Melonie screamed. She clapped her hands over her ears, bolted upright, and opened her eyes all the way. She looked possessed, damaged, like a woman about to die.

Dartanian soothed her. He talked her down, got her to close her eyes and relax, and then counted her back up to consciousness.

"I'm sweating," she said. "What happened? What did I do?"

"You mentioned a preacher."

"Yeah."

"Do you know his name?"

"No. What happened? I'm soaking wet. I'm cold, I'm *cold.* That was a trip!" She brushed her hair back from her forehead. "Welllll . . . did you take advantage of me?"

"Where'd you meet the preacher?"

"Oh, God," she said. "You got a one-track mind."

He questioned her for a half hour before calling a halt. She remembered the preacher but no other details. Dartanian felt good. The break was close. *A preacher who wasn't a preacher,* he thought. Suppose he was a preacher after all? A man like that might have an ax to grind.

The information was inside of her. It would come out. Of that he was certain. Although Dartanian had a competency in hypnosis and interrogation, he wasn't an expert. It was time to call in a mad doctor.

The next morning, a bald man in a brown suit arrived at the East Ninth Street safe house. He had a white beard singed with gray. It was neat and impeccable, culminating in sideburns that were perfectly symmetrical. Dr. Shelley knew his business.

Dartanian introduced him to Melonie and let him do his stuff. He immediately chatted like he was an old friend just dropping in for a visit. He talked about his car, the weather, her hair, and then kissed her hand. "She's even more beautiful than you said, Alex."

Before Melonie had a chance to recover from his bedside manner, he touched her lightly on the shoulders and looked into her eyes. "There's nothing to worry about," he said. "What we're going to do is perfectly normal." She nodded and smiled.

Accustomed to a life where normal was a negotiable term, Melonie wasn't worried by his presence.

Dr. Shelley's charm would have been exactly the same had he been there to waste Melonie. He was a contract agent for the intelligence community. His past in military intelligence covered two wars. His behavorial modification experiments were sponsored by Ivy League universities and think tanks. Shelley was in demand. He commanded a high price, but he earned it.

After talking with her for a half hour, Shelley described everything he was going to do so that she wouldn't panic. First, he put her into a light trance. He injected her with enough sodium pentathol to knock her out. Unlike hypnosis, where the subject maintained a degree of awareness, narcotherapy crashed down the walls of consciousness. It depended on creating a series of illusions. The operator tricked the subject into reliving the event by posing as one of the participants. He then guided the hallucinogenic trance state wherever he wanted it.

Dr. Shelley gave her a second shot ten minutes later. This time it was a wake-up hit of benzine to restore her vocal ability.

Dartanian felt the break more than yesterday. Shelley's manner was such that he wouldn't accept defeat. It was going to happen. He watched the beautiful "knockout" respond to Shelly's questions. He quickly convinced her that he was one of her friends walking beside her on the day she met the preacher.

"Where will we meet the preacher?" he asked.

"Carnival," she said. "Going to the carnival."

"Where is it?"

"Nowhere special. Just a carnival that came to Boston."

She took Shelley to the tent where they listened to the preacher.

"What's his name?"

"Lockwood," she said. "But he's not a preacher."

"Why?"

"He said he's quitting. He tries so hard, but he's so young looking. Look at him! He's a kid, and he's calling us on the carpet. Gotta change our ways. I'm gonna ball him at the motel."

Shelley shared the illusion with her. He became the preacher and went with her to the motel. Melonie talked about the commune staying at the run-down haven. Then, she talked about the movie.

"I'm taking part in a sex film?" Shelley asked, assuming Lockwood's role.

"Mmmmmmm. Have some coke, tiger."

"I'm a preacher. Why am I letting someone film me with you?"

"You're not a preacher any more. You're Tim Lockwood, and right now the only thing you care about is getting your rocks off."

"Where can I get the film?" Shelley asked.

"Ask Freddy for a copy. He's the one making it. He's a pack rat. He keeps everything. Don't you, Freddy?"

"What's Freddy's last name?"

"You're dumb, aren't you? Dumb but cute."

"What's his name?"

"Freddy Cantor," she said.

"Where can I find him?"

The Merchant Street offices of WBLZ in Boston were tucked behind a tragic stone face that looked like the Alamo just after the attack. Inside, it was modern, but the gloomy first impression hung on.

Dartanian had shaken off the inertia from the flight to Boston International and the ride to the television studio. He stopped at the glassed-in reception cubicle on the first floor.

A white-haired woman in a queen-sized green dress reluctantly left her typing to come to the window. She lost her scowl the moment she saw the striking blond-haired man waiting for her. His piercing blue eyes, strong jaw, and powerful build made her wish she could drop 30 years from her age.

"Yes? How can I help you?"

Dartanian smiled and guided her eyes to the counter between them. He opened his trifold to show a detective's shield. It was a New York badge for a nonexistent cop, but she didn't look close. A nice man like this would never be an imposter. "I'm here to see Freddy Cantor," he said.

"Oh gosh, officer, I'm so sorry. Mr. Cantor never sees anyone this close to a news broadcast."

On his way to becoming news director for WBLZ, the former cameraman and porn producer had dropped the "Freddy" and gained a "Mister." Dartanian glanced at the wall clock above her. It was 5:45, 15 minutes until the news. He leaned close and whispered. "His life may be in danger, Ma'am." *From me.*

Her face brightened. "An emergency? In that case, you just go right down that hall."

Dartanian walked to a metal door at the end of a thin corridor. A buzzer sounded, and the lock clicked open. Three doors down was the corner office of Mr. Cantor. He'd just hung up the phone when Dartanian entered.

"What's this about an emergency?" he said. His shirt sleeves were rolled to the elbow. A blue tie hung loosely around his neck, and his drinker's face was hidden by dark sunglasses. He lifted the shades for a better look at the newcomer. His eyes were bleary.

"I'm here for a pornography film you made a long time ago," Dartanian said.

"Who are you?"

"Cooperate and you won't have to find out."

"I never did any porn."

"Looks like you gotta find out." He closed the door and hurried to the desk before Cantor had a chance to pick up the phone. Dartanian pushed aside a stack of newspapers. The *Boston Herald* tabloid laid on top of the *Boston Globe* and *Hartford Courant*. Cantor had been doing some last-minute searching for news to recycle.

Dartanian planted his right palm on the center of the desk. He wagged his left index finger in front of Cantor's nose. "Smart people don't fuck with me."

Cantor backed away like the finger was a snake about to strike. Dartanian knew he'd chosen the right tactic. If he came in and waffled about looking for old porn films, posing as a collector, Cantor would have given him the runaround. It was better to come on as a hard guy. A crazy hard guy.

"You're too late," Cantor said, admitting obliquely that he'd been in the porn field.

Dartanian froze him with a glare, making him speak.

"I got pushed out of the business five years ago," Cantor whined. "Guys like you came in and steamrolled me. They made me sell all my films. Gone, every last one of them."

"Don't lie to me, Mr. Freddy Cantor of 993 Chalice Drive. Mr. Freddy Cantor, 45 years old, who drives a black Camaro. Do you understand me, Mr. Freddy Cantor. I know all about you. I can make you vanish."

"Look! I'm telling the truth. What can I do?"

"You can level with me," Dartanian said. "My information tells me that you never let anything go, that you are the type who has dupes of every piece of film he ever made. I'm willing to bet your life on it."

"Maybe."

"Come on," Dartanian said. "Let's go outside."

"You think I'm crazy? I'm not going anywhere with you!" He looked around his office. His eyes darted to every corner, as if he could bring out reinforcements simply by wishing for them to appear.

"I'm not unreasonable," Dartanian said. He took out three hundred-dollar bills and dropped them on the desk. "That's for your film and your time. You're coming with me to your place. And don't worry. I have a friend in the car who's also your friend. Got it? You see who it is, and if you don't want to go, you don't have to. Right?"

Dartanian wasn't about to let him go, even if he didn't like the passenger in the rented car outside the studio. One way or another Cantor was going to deliver the film. Now.

But it was a quiet way of getting him outside. Cantor glanced in the back seat of the rented Buick. "Melonie!" he said. "It's great to see ya . . . but you're keeping such bad company these days."

"Get in," Dartanian said. "You've only seen my good side so far."

* * *

The Wellington, Long Island, Church of Hope wasn't the most exciting location Mick Porter had ever visited. In fact, it was about as exciting as the 100 other churches, fellowships, and backyard congregation halls he'd investigated. He felt like he was going to OD on good will.

This church also served as headquarters for the Interdenominational Peace Project and the World Charity Fund. The Peace Project was a fundamentalist lobbying group that wanted the United States to double their nuclear arms in the next five years. The World Charity Fund had raised millions for food giveaway programs in the last two years. Ninety percent of the money went for in-house administration costs.

The stucco walls of the waiting room lost their fascination after the first half hour. The religious magazines on the marble-capped coffee table were as useless as ladies' magazines. Why couldn't they stock the place with something decent like *Eagle* or *Security World?*

It was stuffy in the room. Only the bottom panels of the stained-glass windows opened. The beautiful sunny day outside belonged to another world. In here a shroud of dusty gloom covered everything.

The worst part about waiting wasn't the heat or the doom. No, the toughest part was waiting with Simara. The slight-looking Japanese man hadn't said more than two words in the past 40 minutes. He sat and breathed deeply like a patient saint. Mick wondered if Simara had sunk into the satori state he was always talking about. *Satori, my ass!* Mick thought. He could almost feel Simara's eyes following him as he paced the room, but every time he looked back Simara gazed straight ahead.

"Do you have to be so damn patient!" Mick roared. "Always acting perfect no matter what we have to do."

"It's my nature," Simara said.

Mick groaned. He'd seen too many of these waiting rooms. Half the time, he was with Simara. The rest of the time they chased separate leads. Now they were down to Reverend Burroughs and the Church of Hope and a few more individuals. Mick had encountered con men, genuine do-gooders, a few radical social workers, and maybe 10 legitimate reverends who'd been connected to the St. Theresa Foundation for the Elderly. It was a hard chain to break. Each lead turned up a few more names, but none of them had direct links to the people behind the foundation. Burroughs was promising, but Mick had chased down too many wrong trails to get excited.

He sat on a low-slung padded bench across from Simara. He looked at his watch. Burroughs was a busy man and Mick had come unannounced, but even so, the reverend promised to meet with him in 10 minutes. That had been almost an hour ago. He was closeted with two of his fund raisers, discussing the holy dollar.

"So what do you think of the Giants?" Mick said.

"I don't think of such things," Simara answered.

"Quit busting my balls, will ya?" Mick said. He wanted action, conversation, anything to get him out of this dim room. A moment later, he almost kissed the middle-aged woman who came in the room.

"Reverend Burroughs will see you now."

They stepped inside an air-conditioned office.

Burroughs was a husky man in a somber suit. He looked like the outdoors type. Mick was perversely glad that he also had to waste a perfect Saturday inside.

"You mentioned donations," Burroughs said. He sat behind the desk with folded hands, ready to count money.

"Yes," Mick agreed. "Your name came up with the St. Theresa Foundation for the Elderly."

Burroughs sat up straight. He wore a guarded look at the mention of the foundation. He waited for more explanation.

"The reason I'm here. . . ." Mick went into his standard spiel about his sick aunt who'd been provided for by the foundation when her money ran out. The imaginary aunt raised him since he was a boy, and he vowed he would repay the foundation for their kindness if he ever had the chance.

"Well, sir," Mick said. "I've done well, and I am prepared to give $100,000 to St. Theresa's organizers. Only trouble is, I can't find them."

Burroughs was hooked. "As you've guessed," he said, "I have done some work for them. Unfortunately, the man behind St. Theresa's wishes to remain anonymous. That's the way he is."

Mick shook his head. "I'm a man of my word. I want to repay him. Now, Reverend Burroughs, I believe the Lord steered me here to you. And I believe it's God's will that you should help me further my quest. Of course, I expect to make a considerable contribution to your Church of Hope here. After all, you too are doing the Lord's work."

"Of course," Burroughs said. "I really shouldn't divulge the information, but since you are a special case. . . ." He looked at Sin Simara with distrust. Like so many other elitist reverends Mick had encountered, Burroughs wasn't too keen on foreigners. Christ died on the cross for white people who lived in the United States. It said so right in the Bible.

"Could we speak in private?" Burroughs asked, noddng toward Simara.

"That's okay," Mick said. "He's just a servant. He doesn't speak English."

"Just to be on the safe side," Burroughs said. He waved Mick into an adjoining office.

The stocky ICE agent hid his impatience and annoyance at the man's pettiness. He was about to get what he'd been searching for. One wrong word or look could blow it.

With a conspiratorial gaze, Reverend Burroughs said, "The man you're looking for is Luke Revere."

"I see. Where can I find him?"

"Luke Revere!" Burroughs said. "And the Ministry of the Air! Surely you've heard of him."

"I'm not too familiar with his operation."

Burroughs rolled his eyes heavenward. "He's the number-one television evangelist in the country! His crusades come through here every year. You see, we are the local pastors and he is the shepherd, and we all get a chance to host one of his broadcasts. It's simply beautiful what we can raise for the Lord. And we get 50 percent of the gate."

Mick hated to cut short the man's religious ecstasy, but he wanted out. "Where can I find him?"

"White Plains," Burroughs said. He spoke like it was the Holy Land.

"Thanks," Mick said and turned to leave.

"Wait! The contribution you mentioned. . . ."

Mick did an about face and pulled a white envelope out of his suit jacket. Burroughs followed him to the next office before opening it.

"Hop to it," Mick yelled to Simara.

Simara pulled a stooge act and instantly jumped to his feet. He fell in behind Mick Porter and turned back at the door to see Reverend Burroughs holding a five-dollar bill in his hand like a dead rat.

Nine

Deacon Archer swung the KG9 machine pistol from his hip and strafed the grassy knoll. A beer can pyramid exploded 40 yards in front of him. He laughed and shoved another clip into the futuristic blaster. "Pull!" he shouted.

A mountain man in baggy jeans tossed a full beer can into the air.

Archer zapped it with a full clip. Jets of foam whooshed from all sides. "Top that, motherfucker," he said. He set his weapon on a tree stump and popped the tab on another beer. The tall muscled deacon chugged it like it was a thimbleful. Beer splattered his bare chest. He grabbed a cold beer from the cooler at his feet. "Ready when you are, Magyar," he dared.

Magyar wobbled to his feet. He grinned like a drunken loon. Alcohol sweat ran down his cheeks to salt his pirate beard. Unlike Archer, his muscles were hidden beneath a shapeless bulk. Magyar was a clay golem dug out of a hillside and clothed in denim.

"Pull!" Magyar roared.

Archer tossed the can in grenade fashion. Magyar's KG9 homed on the missile with drunken radar. He drilled the bottom of the can with a dozen slugs, then disintegrated the spiraling tin with the rest of the clip before it hit the ground.

"Decent," Archer said.

"Decent your ass!" Magyar sputtered. "Better'n you could ever hope for."

Both men knew bikes, guns, and drugs, having dealt them all in the days they road together. That was years ago. This morning was spent in beery nostalgia. They relived the places and faces they'd trashed.

The secluded back acres of the Revere Bible Institute were littered with beer cans, cardboard bull's-eyes, and dead squirrels. Archer thought of the Bible students who used this spot to meditate. The next batch would probably think the "end times" had begun.

It was a nice setting. Deacon Archer often came here by himself to practice with new weapons. All around him were woods and a cold spring. Revere had fençed the entire preserve with black iron spires. In took an army of volunteers one month to get the job done. Volunteers, dummies, cannon fodder. The words were interchangeable as far as Archer was concerned. The dumb animals were too blind to see a con man milking their wallets.

"What you thinking about?" Magyar said. "You gone blank or something?"

Deacon Archer considered sending Magyar away. Some friend he was, inviting Magyar onto a sinking ship. Revere's operation was going to hell. The man was out of control. Still, his only chance of riding away from this depended on recuiting top fighters like Magyar. He flashed on the dope deals, shoot-outs on desolate roads, and the contract one of their burn victims put out on them. Archer and

Magyar suddenly found themselves running from ex-friends turned bounty hunters. They'd saved each other's ass more than once before they separated.

"Come on, man!" Magyar said. "You didn't bring me out here to play with pop guns. What's the deal?"

Archer told him about Revere's hit list, the deacon squads, and how the Revere Institute was the end of the rainbow. "He takes in a pot of gold every week. Only problem is he's crazy. The man's ruining a good thing. Damn hit list grows longer all the time without rhyme or reason."

"Why's he gotta rack up so many bodies?" Magyar asked. He continued to drink, but his eyes came back into focus. This was a business deal.

"That's the million-dollar question," Archer said. "You get the answer when you come in."

"Yeah." Magyar could live without knowing. "Tell me about this deacon business anyway."

Archer nodded. "Revere keeps dossiers on all his followers. He's a sharp dude. He picks out the ones most likely to succeed as martyrs, and grooms them into fanatics. Man, those suckers will do anything. I mean, we're talking crazier than you!"

He explained how Revere created an inner circle within the Ministry. Big contributors or volunteer workers were eligible to become deacons. They handled the everyday details related to Revere's periodic crusades. They traveled with him like unpaid migrant workers; their reward was a special seat in heaven right next to Luke Revere.

Then there were the fighting deacons. Revere pulled their strings. Archer whipped them into shape.

"So how are they?" Magyar asked.

"I trained a dozen groups so far. Knowing Revere, that pecker's probably got a few more stashed for emergencies. Anyway, I came up with some mediocre squads and one elite squad."

"Yeah? Great. So where are the elite?"

"Dead," said Archer. The pain in his eyes wasn't sympathy for the lost. The remaining deacons were fanatics, but they needed a lot more training.

"Really knew their shit, huh?"

"They were good," Archer said. "As good as I could make them. Against normal men, they might've done all right. As it happened, they nailed a good number before they got wasted."

"Who's the competition?"

Deacon Archer described the men who iced every charging fanatic with military precision. "These guys are primo, man. If you had any sense, you'd fight on their side."

Magyar's tired eyes flared with interest. "Really that fucking good, Huh?"

Archer nodded. "I've been casing them out, man. Trying to get a fix on this Melonie chick. She's a porno babe, top of the list."

"My kind of people."

A cold summer breeze rushed through the woods. Both men turned into it to let the beer sweat fly away. Archer leaned back on the stump and flexed his packed muscles the way an animal does. He stretched all seven feet and shuddered.

"Anyway, I figure my chance—maybe *our* chance—is riding on this Dartanian cat. The way I see it, I get him or he gets me. There's no walking away."

"So?" Magyar asked.

"So I'm gonna take him out with the chick, man. Sooner or later, they got to come out for air, and when they do, my people will see it. What the hell, it's time to throw the second string into the game. I'll be the clean-up man."

Magyar dropped his massive bulk to the grass. He stuffed a thin joint in his mouth and looked at the sky. He sucked three tokes while it still flamed. Crackling embers fell onto his moth-eaten shirt and burned right through to the skin. He didn't bother to notice the pain.

He passed the joint to Archer, then pulled it away. "Sorry, man, I forgot. You're pure as the driven snow. *You* don't take drugs."

"Damn right. If you come in with me, you don't take 'em any more either."

"Guess I better finish this little number then," Magyar said. "It's gonna be my last for a while." He toked and held his breath until his lungs fought back. He exhaled and laughed at the same time. "Just like the old days," he said.

Archer smiled. He grabbed the smoldering roach and pinched it out with his finger and thumb. He sprinkled the ashes over Magyar's sprawling body. "Deacon Magyar, you just got ordained. Welcome to the club, motherfucker."

"Welcome to the number-one Christian celebration! Welcome to Luke Revere's Ministry of the air!"

Luke Revere leaped onto the stage while the announcer's echo boomed through the great hall. He skipped and jumped like an athlete warming up for a fight.

The full house of fundamentalists clapped rabidly for Revere, God, and country. They shouted his name when he raised his hands to heaven. In the outside world, a man raving and dancing like Revere would be locked up. In this world, he made an ideal prophet—vibrant, handsome, maniacally ready to deliver the word.

"Hallelujah and God bless you all!" Luke shouted. The applause grew louder. He ran a hand through his slickly coiffed hair and stalked the audience. The hair waved like a lion's mane. This man could move mountains, chase away the devil, and fill you with the spirit in the time it took most people to brush their teeth.

"You're all wonderful! God bless you for coming here today. I *mean* it! God knows I mean it!" The audience preened like 10,000 Pavlovian dogs. They knew what came next. It was stroke time.

"Go on and give yourselves a hand. Let me hear you! Ahhh, that's so fine, so wonderful! Praise God for bringing me so many wonderful Christians today!"

Businessmen, wholesome housewives, dumbstruck teenagers, and blue-haired old ladies blissed out in waves of handclapping that crested on the stage and broke on the broad shoulders of Luke Revere.

Luke fell into his rap. At times, he was unaware of the crowd, totally carried away by the sound of his own voice. It was like someone else was talking and ranting at him, and he was the spectator. He took his cue from the voice and feigned whatever emotion was called for.

Struck with sadness, Luke froze in place. His head jerked heavenward. A hand covered his eyes. Tears ran down his cheeks. Luke Revere was sad, he told the crowd. Even as he looked at so many souls filled with the spirit, he couldn't help thinking of those who didn't have God inside them. "Could be your brother!" he shouted. "Your sister! Couldbeyourmotheryourfather—andmaybeyourbestfriend!" The gasping race-track style was as traditional for a TV evangelist as Johnny Carson's monologue. It gave the impression that God breathed in their lungs and was in a hurry to get out and deliver the message.

Today's message was that God didn't mind if you were rich and couldn't always come to church because you were busy. God understood those things. In fact, God told Luke who shared it with the audience, that there was no reason to feel guilty about being wealthy—as long as you gave a fair share of that wealth to the church.

"You have got to give," Revere pleaded. "You just got to *give.* We allllll got to giiiive!" He wheezed like a dying man. He confronted the audience with his tears. "Don't you see? Don't you see what I'm talking about? It's staring right in front of us. The answer is *give.* Give until it hurts. I know you don't have the time to preach God's word because you got your jobs, you got your family. But I do! I got all the time in the world to preach God. I canpreachtothepeopletwentyfourhoursadaybut-onlyifyouhelp. That's right. It's up to you. It ain't up to me. So what're you gonna do? God's listening. God's waiting for your answer."

There was little sound in the audience. They felt guilty because they had almost made strapping Luke Revere break down in tears because they weren't giving enough to the Ministry. They feasted on the shame.

Revere took a deep breath. *"If you can't give the time, then give the help!"* he hollered.

The first seven rows jerked back like they'd been slapped in the face.

Luke Revere walked the stage and made eye contact with as many of the faithful as he could focus on. He got into it, studying the middle-

American pie dumped into his hall waiting to be sliced. The coke rushed him from stage left to stage right and then made him pace the center. Damn, that girl in the front row had nice tits! Nice legs. Nice yellow dress. 18 or 19 years old. Who the fuck could tell these days? But God, did she have nice tits! How did he miss her before when he scanned the audience monitor in his chapel?

Uh-oh, something was wrong. His announcer, Ted Grant, was staring at him from the wings. Grant was part Howdy Doody, part Ed MacMahon. He helped out with the Johnny Carson portion of the show when Luke interviewed people who donated money to the Ministry and got it back tenfold from the Lord's bank account. Howdy Doody actually believed in Revere. He chuckled at all his jokes and said "Praise God" every 45 seconds. But something was wrong with Howdy. His cherubic face gave way to anger. Or was it worry? He was staring at Revere like Revere had done something wrong.

The coke paranoia multiplied into a thousand silent screams. The audience was staring at him. *What did I do?* They were all shell-shocked. Shit, how long had he been standing here like a blank? Or did he say something? *Oh fuck, I must have said nice tits out loud. That's why they're staring. I blew it.* He thought of all the coke-outs he'd had off stage. He finally waltzed into psychosis right in front of the damned faithful.

He had to say something to pull this one out of the fire. Instinct took over. He pivoted to his left and slashed his arm in the air. He pointed toward the ceiling.

"God has just spoken to me!" he said to the audience. "As I stand before you, he has spoken to me, and you all know that when God speaks you listen no matter where you are or what you're doing—even if you're preaching to 16 million people at the time. All of you who are saved know what it's like when he speaks."

The heads bobbed like plastic doggies in the back window of 57 Chevies.

"You know what he said to me?" Luke paused for a moment and grabbed the first lunacy that passed through his mind. "God said to me that we are like a farm team and pretty soon we're gonna be harvested to the major leagues. We got to get ready. Got to get into training if we want to make it to God's A team! He wants this ministry to grow."

He looked at the well-dressed marks to judge their response. Good, they were smiling. He'd learned long ago that he could say the most asinine thing and no one would ever call him on it. Bless the ignorant, for they shall make Luke a rich man.

"So come on! Let's get out of that dugout and get onto the playing field! Let's give!"

Sweat darkened his white shirt. It poured down his mane of brown hair onto his cheeks. He took long, deep breaths for the benefit of the audience. Luke was tired. He'd just batted a triple for God. Now it was up to the faithful to beat Satan's team and knock in that winning run.

"We're going to take a short break before we get to the second part of our show. Now, I'm not going to tell you what to give during the break, but if you could see it in your heart to raise your pledges by a small token, even if it's only five dollars a week, well, praise God, the Ministry can keep on going. God bless you all. Come on down to the tables up front and show God that you *can* give till it hurts. Our volunteers will take your pledges. Thank you and praise God."

Luke's slow exit was accompanied by swelling organ music. He hated the cathedral sound, but it reinforced the audience's delusion that they were in a genuine church.

The herd bucked from their seats to take part in the holy sacrament of giving money.

Sin Simara was the last to enter the meeting room on the third floor of the safe house. Tim Reed and Mick Porter sat across from each other at a long oval conference table. Dartanian stood at the far end behind a projector and a carton of films. A videocassette deck sat next to the projector.

"Seen any good films lately?" Simara said.

"This one's a killer," Dartanian said. He threaded a Super-8mm reel onto the projector. Simara pulled up a chair next to Mick and looked at the white screen on the wall. Dartanian dimmed the lights and switched on the projector.

A beacon of light splashed onto the screen. The projector breathed loud for several seconds. Then Melonie appeared. She was younger but just as appealing. Naked and stoked with drugs and passion. The camera shot up to the man's face.

"That's Tim Lockwood on the receiving end," Dartanian said. He blew smoke into the projector beam. "At the time, he was a preacher. He told Melonie he was giving it up." He froze the film with a close-up of the man's face.

He pushed a tape into the VHS unit wired to a widescreen television at the end of the table. The screen showed a man in a brown suit dashing across a stage. Even though the volume was low, his ranting voice demanded attention. "God does know what you give to the Ministry! $10, $50, $100—he keeps track of it all. So start your account with Jesus today *and collect interest for all eternity!*"

"That's Tim Lockwood ten years later. Only now he goes by the name of Luke Revere." Dartanian's neutral voice wavered slightly. His blue eyes knifed the preacher's image.

Mick Porter, Sin Simara, and Tim Reed looked at the two images of Luke Revere. They saw a dead man. There was a tense atmosphere in the room that each man had felt before. The break had taken longer than usual, but it finally had come. From here on, it was steamroller time. The enemy was known, and DSS could fade out.

ICE flowed in their veins.

"Revere is older, filled out some, and obviously he stayed in the preacher business. He covered his past by taking the paper trip. Instead of changing his name legally, he manufactured a totally new identity. With enough money a man can prove he's Daffy Duck if he wants to."

The ICE computer showed that Tim Lockwood had dropped out of sight shortly after the pornographic film was made. Luke Revere's Ministry had begun that same year. They might still be looking for a man named Lockwood if Mick Porter and Sin Simara hadn't traced two of the assassins to Luke Revere via the St. Theresa Foundation.

Taken separately, Revere's connection to assassins and his appearance in a pornography film weren't proof of his involvement. Together, they spelled guilt to all but the blind. Unfortunately, the law was blind. The police could investigate, but Revere would walk away. Millions of dollars and powerful friends would see to that. The killers would sink out of sight.

"We've got all the proof *we* need," Dartanian said. "Who is in a better position than Revere to develop a team of fanatics? The men who came at us on the street were definitely looking to die."

"When do we take him?" Mick asked.

"Not just him," Dartanian said. "Before we move on him, I want tactical intelligence on his White Plains operation. Hundreds of people work for him. They can't all be hitters, but I'm damn sure we'll find enough of them hiding behind his robes. We are going to throw down the guilty."

Dartanian handed a black folder to each man. "Here's the background on Revere. The CIA had a file on him all along. It was part of a research program on cults and their potential use for population control. Revere and a half-dozen other sleazy preachers were included."

The ICE agents scanned the CIA printout. Although the file didn't specifically call Revere an outright crook, the information reinforced the probability that he was the man behind the killings.

Other potential candidates from Melonie's past didn't have the personality or the motives that Revere did. The celebrities tied to Melonie looked on it as a scandalous honor. The political fat cats that shared her bed were has-beens now. She was no threat to them.

She *was* a threat to a man who ran a multimillion dollar empire based on fundamentalist beliefs, with an emphasis on stamping out porn.

"All because of that film with Melonie," Simara said. "Looks like the holy rollers have a new war cry."

"What's that?" Mick asked.

"Oral sex leads to mass murder. They'll play this up for centuries."

"Bizarre," Dartanian agreed. "But in this case, it's true. Mick, I want you to get the film transferred to videotape. Make enough duplicates to send to every major newspaper and television station in the country."

"Immediate release?" Mick asked.

"No," Dartanian said. "First, we'll use it as a sword to wave over his head. We'll bring it down soon enough. For now, let's go over his file to see what breed of bastard we're dealing with."

The CIA file on Revere showed a textbook case on how to run a phony religion. More than a half hour of every Ministry of the Air's broadcast hour was directed to fund-raising activities. Some of it was outright solicitation. Other techniques were subtler. His favorite was to advertise the Revere Bible College by interviewing one of the students and painting a rosy picture for his future. Not only did Revere solicit donations for the unaccredited college, but he snared recruits with his smooth pitch. Revere got the student to praise his "hands-on" experience in his chosen field—which came to approximately 45 hours a week of free labor.

CIA analysis showed Revere's followers came from four groups: grief-stricken people vulnerable to Revere's promises of special prayers that reached God faster than light; people looking for a WASP Utopia that would be spared Armageddon if they stuck with Luke Revere; naive souls taken in by the preacher's charisma; and middle-class people willing to pay a surrogate to take care of their religious obligations.

The Revere Institute's labor practices were illegal outside of religious circles. Like cultists, his followers worked for nothing. They turned over tremendous sums to the church from their fund-raising activities.

A thirst for power led Revere on a private crusade to sink his hooks into senators and congressman across the United States. Although he was based in New York, satellite broadcasts took him to every state in the union. Regional branches of the Ministry politely extorted favorable legislation and funds from the politicians. Revere's payback was a promise to deliver huge blocs of votes to the most generous lawmaker.

Those politicians who refused to knuckle under to Revere were put on the "hit list" and smeared during his broadcasts.

The file covered Revere's hushed-up scandals within the Ministry. His fondness for young followers often resulted in rumors that most followers found hard to believe. Singly, they were deniable. When his escapades were collected over a period of years, he was shown to be a modern-day Casanova.

Aside from his personal weaknesses, Revere's associates within the Ministry were more damning. He worked closely with an inordinate number of former criminals. Peggy Revere had been involved in muggings. Deacon Archer had been embroiled in drugs, weapons sales, and murder. He now served as a bodyguard and bag man for Revere.

The CIA file ended with an appraisal of Revere's skills with mind-control techniques, using fundamentalist fears as a springboard for manipulation of his audience. Revere hid his power-and-money grabbing ego behind a campaign against humanism and that "new permissiveness" that had served preachers so well for the past 20 years.

Revere's organization was a perfect vehicle for

laundering money and influencing public opinion. It could be infiltrated and controlled, perhaps even using Revere as a Company friend. The agent who compiled the report recommended further investigation into Revere's hazy past. There were bound to be more skeletons in the organization than the surface investigation showed, he wrote.

"That's putting it mildly," Dartanian said. "Let's go out there and do our job, gentlemen, so there won't be anything left to investigate."

Tim Reed stayed behind to guard Melonie. Simara and Porter accompanied Mick to Cage Street headquarters. There Dartanian pointed out a shaggy biker hanging loose at the corner. "He's been trying to tail me for two days now," he said.

"You want me to discourage him?" Mick asked.

"No," Dartanian said. "I'm going to use him to hook a few more fish."

"Yeah?" Simara asked. "What are you using for bait?"

Dartanian smiled. "A real live one," Dartanian said. "With plenty of lures."

Ten

Stiletto heels struck the damp sidewalk. A blond woman in a white strapless dress strutted from the shadow of a hangar-shaped warehouse. Sequins sparkled on the red summer wrap that crisscrossed her breasts. She walked into the glare of a street-lamp. The steep heels exaggerated the Marilyn Monroe sway of her hips.

Dartanian glided to her side. He looked down the short block that ended in a yard of truck bodies and construction equipment. He glanced in the other direction. Nothing moved by the Hudson. They were alone at the rain-calmed waterfront. The night belonged to them.

Marilyn Monroe's twin skirted a deep puddle midway to the Audi 5000 at the curb. It was the third night in a row that she followed the same routine with Dartanian.

"Hold it," he said. "I forgot something."

"Oh, hurry up!" she whined. She pouted beneath the light with her hands folded under the wrap. The haughty blond was every inch an impatient prima donna.

Dartanian vanished inside the warehouse. Seconds later a light shimmered in one of the offices.

Footsteps sounded in the distance. First they were stealthy. Then they became frenzied. The pack was on the move. "Oh God!" the blond cried. She stared at the dark yard, frozen like Bambi in a forest crawling with deer jackers.

The shadows took form. Two stocky men raced down the sidewalk from the end of the block. One man screamed an unintelligible war cry. They were going to hit her before Dartanian came back.

Middle-aged crazy men thundered toward her. They might have been harmless commuters running for a train, ties flapping and jackets billowing, if it hadn't been for the KG9 pistols slapping out of their holsters.

"Harlot, harlot, harlot, harlot," the closer man gasped. He paced himself with the word like it was a mantra powering his furious legs.

"Die! Now, now, now!" The second man slammed to a halt. His shoes smacked the cement like the crack of a baseball bat. Both men killed her with their eyes. In chorus, they leveled the blasters.

She startled them with a nightmarish scream. It was their nightmare. The sequined wrap snapped free and drifted to the ground in a slow whirl. She squeezed the Ingram M11 machine pistol in her manicured hands. Twenty rounds of .380 ACP slugs buttoned their chests. The attackers went down like trees felled by an ax.

Two more shapes hurtled toward her. She kicked off her party doll heels and ducked into the shadows. By the time she reached the warehouse wall, she had another clip in the Ingram. Not that she needed it.

One shot rang out at the end of the warehouse. A death scream chased the echo of the bullet. The backup squad was halved. The remaining man changed his direction. Instead of charging the "helpless" woman, he ran from the battlefield.

Dartanian tracked him with the modified nightscope on the Valmet M78. The man scurried over concrete blocks and small piles of copper tubing. He kept his head low. Dartanian targeted him every step of the way, meaning to take him down with a leg shot. This man was going to talk.

The Odin International light machine gun had already done its work. Since the moment he stepped inside the warehouse, Dartanian had manned the station at the far end. He could have taken the first two hitters, but he knew Val Wagner could stand up to them. The raven-haired ICE agent had disguised herself as Melonie Grand with a blond wig and a slinky dress. Her figure matched the starlet's enough to lure the attackers to a date with Val's Ingram M11.

She had held her ground long enough for the backup squad to come into play. Now Dartanian had to make the last move. Finally, the man reached a clear space. Perfect, Dartanian thought. One wounded prisoner coming up. He scoped the runner in the green screen, eased the sight a few paces ahead, breathed out, and pulled the trigger. *Shit,* he thought in that eternal millesecond after he committed himself. The man stumbled head first into the trajectory of the leg shot. The crack of the 7.62 Nato round echoed. *Another dead sonofabitch.*

Dartanian pushed the open window all the way up and sat on the sill. He dropped eight feet to the cement. The Valmet M78 sniffed low to the ground as he went to confirm the kill. The first man he'd shot was curled in a U-shaped position on the sidewalk. The 7.62 Nato slug drilled him through the heart.

Val shouted, "Gone for good! Both of them."

He nodded. That made a definite three. He covered the ground quickly and silently. A moment later he stood over the lifeless body of the second man. What was left of his face laid awkwardly on a pillow of dirt. It was a real horror show. Poor dumb bastard, he thought. He picked up the fallen man's KG9 and joined Val back on the warehouse walk.

She could tell the fourth man was dead by the look on his face.

"What now?" she asked. "We still don't have anyone to interrogate."

"These guys were religious, remember." He looked them over. Val's two were leaking like sieves. The man further down the sidewalk only had one hole in him. "I guess we're just gonna bring one of them back to life."

She followed him to the fresh corpse. The man was close to forty. He had a half smile on his face. In his last moment he'd probably thought he was going straight to heaven, courtesy of Luke Revere's good word. Dartanian checked him to make sure he had a wallet with ID. "Welcome back," Dartanian said. "Mr. Daniel E. Benton, you are about to serve the human race for real."

"What good is it?" Val asked. She scanned the darkness for any more assassins while she talked. It was a natural act for her. She was always on alert.

Dartanian stood up. "Revere sent four men after you, thinking he was gunning down Melonie. Well, in the morning he's going to hear on the news that three men died in a shoot-out. *What happened to the fourth man? The fourth man will vanish.* And Revere will think he's spilling everything he knows."

"Still," Val said. "I don't see how it helps much."

"It helps, all right," Dartanian said. "This Lazarus act is only one part of the game plan. It's time to bring out the dirty tricks."

Her eyes sparked. "I thought this *was* one of the tricks. Dressing up like Melonie while someone tails us qualifies as a dirty trick in my book."

"Read a new one," Dartanian said. "This was just a warm-up." He stared at her as if he'd just noticed the way she was dressed for the first time all night. The cleavage was stunning, as were her sparkling cat's eyes. "God, you look nice tonight. The Ingram becomes you."

Val laughed. She blew imaginary smoke from the barrel of the machine pistol, then tucked it into the side holster that had been hidden by the sequined wrap.

"They should've known better," Dartanian said. "Never trust a woman dressed like that."

She looked into the blond man's eyes. The clear blue made her shudder. Everything about him made her shudder. "If I didn't know better," she said, "I'd think you were getting ready to put the moves on me."

"It's been a long time," he said.

"Mmmmmn," she responded. "It's your move, captain." The damp summer night chilled her flesh and made the goosebumps rise on her bare arms.

Dartanian smiled. Her beauty transported him from the blood bath at their feet to a place of warmth and pleasure that he rarely had time to visit. They had stood together tonight. Now perhaps they would lie together—if the task at hand didn't wreck the electricity passing between them.

"Give me a hand with him," Dartanian said.

She stared at the Benton corpse. "This is a $200 dollar dress."

"Right," Dartanian answered. "A $200 dress on a million dollar body. But the body belongs to an ICE agent. Give me a hand."

"The things we do for love," she said.

Mick Porter wore a green khaki short-sleeve shirt and light cotton pants. It was a gentle summer day, and the streets of the South Bronx were teeming with people looking for something to do, someone to hassle.

He passed the 44th Precinct station house on Sedgwick Avenue. Mick felt sorry for the cops who worked there. They were outmanned and outgunned. For two years in a row, the murder toll in the 44th was the highest in the city, and it was getting worse with each passing day. The streets were full of cheap gunmen with expensive guns.

There were street gangs who watched Mick as he walked through their turf, but no one challenged him. He wore his *fuck with me and you're dead* look.

The dangerous neighborhood was home for Reverend John Soames, a black preacher with a movable church. Mick had checked three locations. Each time he'd found that Soames had moved on.

He finally caught up with him in an abandoned luncheonette off Webster Avenue. The black preacher looked over his shoulder when Mick stepped through the open glass door. He shouted a warm "Hello" and continued peeling yellowed and cracked linoleum from the floor.

"Are you John Soames?"

"Yes. And you are?"

"I'm a friend."

"Well friend, could you help me tear up this floor?"

Mick laughed. He knelt and tore up several squares.

"Getting the church ready," Soames said. "Stead of breakfast, this place gonna serve the Lord come Sunday. You coming?"

He grunted. Soames looked sideways at him. The black man scratched his left temple and wiped sweat from his forehead into his short curly gray hair. His face was lined with other people's troubles. He was tired, but he was the kind of man who never stopped. Mick looked around and saw the piles of linoleum ready for the heap. He'd probably been working for hours.

"So what brings you here on a Saturday?" Soames asked.

A CIA file and a murderous shaman, Mick thought. "Can I be straight with you?" he asked.

"You better."

"Can you tell me why you sit at Luke Revere's prayer breakfast every Sunday when you are the last person in the world to belong there?"

"Now how'd you find that out?"

Mick kept working beside the preacher. "Is it true?"

"It is."

"Why?"

"It's my cross to bear," Soames said. "Know thine enemy. And take what scraps you can."

"Revere helps your church," Mick said. "No wonder you got so many troubles."

The black man nodded. "He helps, but never enough. And what he does give, he makes sure the world hears about it. But when I need him most, when the church is going under, he doesn't want to hear about it."

"Why does he bother in the first place? And why are you part of the caucus with those hustlers?" Except for Soames, there were no ordained ministers at Revere's gatherings. "Half of those sleazoids are heading for the pen."

"I'm the token black," Soames said. "And the token poverty case. He gets two in one for his publicity show."

"You could quit going."

"Could. But I won't. You see, these kind of preachers are stealing the souls and the money away from real churches, and no one fights them. They are too powerful. But Reverend John W. Soames is gonna fight them and win. I'm picking up on everything Revere does. And I'm gonna take him down from the inside. In the meantime, he give me just enough rent for this castle." Soames paused. He stopped working at the floor for the first time. "Now suppose you tell me your interest in me and him and how you know what you know."

"We're on the same side in this one," Mick said. "I want to expose him. I need all the information about him. I need his hopes, dreams, and his fears. And I need you to talk to me."

"I want to get to know you better before we get down to tacks. Let's start tomorrow."

"Sure," Mick agreed. "What time?"

"Service starts at seven. Get here a little early, and you can help me set up."

The next morning found Mick sitting among ninety of Soames' parishioners. They were mostly black, with a few whites scattered through the folding chairs that served as pews. Mick only expected to put in his time to humor Soames, but he found himself caught up in the man's sermon.

Soames didn't rant or rave. He just talked. He talked loud and he made sense, and that was the last thing Mick expected to find in a church. He'd been exposed to so many charlatans and sleazy preachers on the trail that led to Revere that he forgot true ministers existed.

"The problem is . . ." Soames paused at the front of the congregation and looked in the face of each member. His own ebony face nodded up and down, counting heads. "The problem is that we can't get enough people to come out and praise the Lord today. Nowadays people are staying inside to get their religion. They get it from Tee Vee! And they get it while they sipping their coffee and munching their breakfast, and then they flip the channel to watch Brady Bunch reruns. And if you ask me, that's a step up from the canned goods the Tee Vee preachers are selling!"

Soames spoke about Revere and the other electronic pitchmen and how they were actually destroying the Christian structure they claimed to rescue. Mick thought it was a miracle that Revere gave any money to Soames, considering the message Soames delivered. But then, Revere probably thought Soames was inconsequential. Revere reached millions. Soames was fighting to keep less than a hundred members together.

"So what happens," Soames said, "is that we don't see each other anymore. We stay inside and we send money to the Tee Vee church, and we wait for a receipt in the mail for buying a ticket into heaven. Well, you can't buy a ticket, and you can't sit back and think you doing your share, and you don't get into heaven 'cause some sucker pulled the wool over your eyes. The preachers tell you to vote for Senator So-and-So, and I have to ask you, what does that have to do with God. You don't sell your vote just like you don't sell your soul."

Soames wrapped up his sermon with a plea to help with several church projects that were drying up for lack of money and volunteers.

After the service, the parishioners came up front to talk with Soames. Instead of giving, they got. He arranged food and a place to stay for those who needed it.

Mick was the last to leave the makeshift church. He made an appointment to pick Soames' brain the following day. At the door, Mick looked over his shoulder. "By the way," he said. "Are you going to Revere's powwow today?"

"Yes. I know. You want me to do you a favor and keep your visit a secret."

"No," Mick said. "Do me a favor. *Tell* Revere someone was asking about him."

Luke Revere was terribly silent. Rage contorted his face. His cheeks were red and specked with sweat even with the chapel's air conditioning set high.

Cocaine screwed him to the leather chair behind the video-control lectern. He'd just finished watching a copy of the porno tape that came in the package earlier today. It was the one that featured Melonie Grand going down on him. The tape that he'd killed for was back in circulation. This one had been altered at the end, however. There was a message printed across the screen right after his image vanished.

SHAME ON TIM LOCKWOOD, the message read.

SHAME ON LUKE REVERE. FOR YOUR PENANCE, TAKE TWENTY SLUGS AND GO TO HELL.

Mad energy boiled through him, but it had nowhere to exit. He was too stunned to vent his rage. For once in his life, Luke Revere was struck dumb.

Deacon Archer sat on the golden railing in front of Revere's glittering altar. He wore a denim work shirt cut off at the sleeves, black pants, and nut-busting boots. Archer looked as much in place in the chapel as a rat in a Waldorf salad. His ox-muscled arms gripped the railing as he watched Revere crack up.

Peggy Revere paced the chapel, stealing pensive looks at Revere. She wore her beautiful loyal-wife mask. Peggy would stand by her man until the chips were down. Then she would help push him off the cliff. The preacher's wife wore a form-fitting cotton dress and flashed painted eyes at her troubled husband.

More than the tape bothered him. The package sent to Revere included Daniel Benton's wallet. A circled newspaper item showed that three men were killed in a waterfront shootout. *Three* men. Revere had sent *four* deacons. He had to assume that Benton was alive and squealing.

Another newspaper had a story in the gossip column about rumors that a porno tape linking Melonie Grand and a well-known evangelist was showing up around town.

"They're killing me," Revere finally said. "They're fucking killing me! All that I've worked for. They're gonna tear it down!"

"Calm down," Archer suggested.

"What? Are you crazy? This is the end, and you tell me to calm down. Dammit, those bastards are all over. They even got to Soames. Some guy's asking all sorts of questions about me. And what about all those strange cars roaming around outside the gate, huh? What about that? They're getting ready to roll over us!"

The man was falling apart at the worst possible time, Archer thought. *It could have been so good.* Archer had recruited real fighters from his outlaw past. Five of them were cooped up in a wing of the Institute with a hooker and a case of beer at this very moment. The other deacons were taking shape. Archer drilled the hell out of them day after day. So what if they lost a few every now and then. There were plenty more to work with. To top things off, Archer had his old buddy Magyar riding with him again.

Archer's troops were ready to fight a pitched battle, ready to win, *dammit*—if Revere didn't drown in his misery. "This ain't doing neither of us any good," Archer said. "You gotta pull yourself together, man."

"Shut up!" Revere shouted. "You are nothing. You don't know what's at stake here. You don't know how long it took to build, and now it's all ruined."

Peggy sought to comfort Luke. She crept up behind him and massaged his shoulders. "Poor baby," she said. "You should listen to Archer—"

Revere slapped her face. The backhanded blow jerked her neck back before she fell. Knucklemarks blossomed on her cheek. "You keep it shut too, bitch!" he seethed. "You're worthless. What have you done for me? Nothing!" He lunged down and hit her again.

That's no punishment, Deacon Archer thought. *She likes it.* Archer rushed forward. He caught Revere's fist before it came down again. He didn't really care if he destroyed her. But not now and not here. Things were bad enough already. There was no need to call any more attention to themselves. Revere strained, intent on smashing Peggy one more time. Archer held him with no effort. "Back off," Archer warned.

Revere's wide eyes snapped back to reality. He relaxed his fist, and Archer let him go. Peggy backed away on the floor. She didn't say a word. She smoothed her hair and tried a smile on her mad king of a husband.

"Decide, baby," Archer said. "We're gonna fight this out as one big happy family, or I split tonight."

"How can we fight?" Revere said. "They know who we are now. They'll bring in cops."

Archer laughed. "Cops! You shitting me? These guys don't truck with cops, man. They want to take care of business. And we're the business."

Revere shook his head. He was looking for an excuse to give in rather than fight. The temptation to run was overwhelming.

"They're gonna carve up the empire, man," Archer said. "Wham! You're old history. They bring in a new guy and pull his strings. They live in your castle, baby."

Revere smiled. He recognized when someone was trying to manipulate him. But even so, it worked. Archer made sense. Why give it up on a platter?

"All right," Revere said. "But pass the word to start liquidating some of our holdings. I want cash available if this doesn't work out."

"Whatever you say." Archer nodded his head. He smiled at the jittery preacher. "But let me clue you in, man. If this doesn't work out, we won't be needing any money. Cash ain't worth a fiddler's fuck in hell."

Eleven

The white Rolls idled softly at the curb. Peggy Revere stepped out of the back seat and waved the driver on. Her red hair hid beneath a platinum page-boy wig. Pearls dipped into her blouse and a gold necklet glistened around her throat. The slave look made her extremely noticeable, although the only thing she was enslaved to was money. That made her subject to Luke Revere's every whim and command.

She could pull it off, she thought when she entered the Clover Patch on Third Avenue. She'd done it before often enough. A kiss of excitement swept over her when she saw him.

The blond target sat at the farthest booth at the back of the club. He watched her look about for a place to sit. His eyes caught hers twice. She smiled the second time. He nodded.

She hustled her expensively wrapped ass down the cool dark lane between the bar and the booths. Professional types looked her way as she passed. She heard comments about her body and her gorgeous silvery hair. Peggy didn't look at anyone except the man in the blue suit at the end.

"Care for some conversation?" she asked. She caressed the leather top of the seat facing him.

"Whatever you say."

She tucked her skirt behind her when she sat. He ordered her a drink. He looked at the splendid breasts dancing in the filmy blouse when she laughed. She laughed a lot. She reached across the table and toyed with his hands like a fortune teller. Contact was the key to it all.

He was a pushover. She fought back the urge to laugh at him. This was the man her husband feared. This was the man who had big bad Archer on the run. This man was hers. He was no different when it came to the weakness of the flesh. His weakness, her flesh. He was about to get fucked into the next life.

Peggy stroked the stem of her wine glass. She drained the last two sips of the Campari and tongued the inside swell of the glass. Her fluttering, glossy fingernails combed the bangs of the page-boy wig.

Come on, honey, take the bait. Take me home. She felt the special sensation that always came before a victory. Her knees pressed together. She sat up straight in the seat. He bought her another drink and ordered another bottle of Grolsch for himself. *Get loose, baby, get loose. Let me give it to you.*

Conversation flowed off her tongue like honey. She had lived so many lies and played so many games that she could become any person she wanted and more important, any person *he* wanted. She played a fast-track career woman for him. A professional management training instructor, she told him. She was here in New York to run a seminar for corporate executives moving into upper management.

"It's a wonderful experience," she said. "But it's *sooo* much pressure on me! I just need a release before I go mad." Her fingers wrung some more foreplay from the wine stem.

He bought it. She could see it in his eyes. *Mmmmmmn, I'm gonna take you apart.* Her toe brushed his leg. "Sorry," she said. She did it again. He smiled. It made her shiver. The man was striking. His deep blue eyes and his strong jaw affected her. If she had normal cravings, this would be for her. She could feel the power inside him, even sitting across the table from him.

But the power was about to go out. It was easier than she expected, but she was a pro. She knew how to tug a man's lust out into the open. It was instinct. He had been seen in the Clover Patch two nights in a row. One of the deacons followed him inside. After tonight, he would be seen no more.

"Oh, but I've been doing all the talking," she said. "I didn't give you a chance to tell me about yourself. Come on, let me have it. What do you do?"

"I'm in information systems," he said.

"What kind?" she asked. "It sounds so exciting."

"All kinds. We do a lot of tracking. A lot of analysis. Anything a computer can do, we're involved. It's not really that interesting."

My cover's better than yours, she thought. He'd fallen for hers. She could see it in his eyes. He was getting hungry. She steered the conversation back to her need for release. The next thing she mentioned was the hotel she was staying at. "It's just down the street."

"Shall we go?" He escorted her down the bar, past the men who'd wished for her before. They ogled her again, but this time they didn't make any comments. The blond man had that effect on people.

Five minutes later, they were in her room at the Markham Hotel. She turned on the bedside stereo and dimmed the lights. It was shadowy and romantic. She pretended to be a drunk, desirable woman who had to be humored or else her mood would go down in flames.

"Dance with me," she said.

He laid his cigarette in the slot of a five-starred ashtray on the dresser. She floated to him and wrapped his hands around her. He held her loosely around the small of her back.

"Uh-uh," she said. She pushed his hands down to the full curves of her ass.

Without much effort, her blouse came off. Her bra straps dropped down her shoulders. She pressed her creamy flesh against him and forgot all about dancing.

They fell onto the bed when they were naked. She gasped at the scars and ran her fingers over his chest. Her mouth followed her fingers. As she moved down, her breasts rolled over his stomach, hips, and then covered his stiff member. "Ooooooh," she murmured. She shimmied from left to right and then sank her mouth onto him. *Enjoy it while you can,* she thought. My turn comes next. She dropped her right hand over the edge to lift the satin bedspread. She parted the mattress and boxspring until her fingers curled around the black metal hilt of a dagger.

"Close your eyes, baby," she cooed. "Let me take care of you right. Just lie there and relax."

He closed his eyes and breathed softly.

The knife swung over her head. She slammed

the heel of her palm under his chin and pushed up. The knife came down.

Dartanian let it fall. At the last possible instant, he shot his left hand up. He gripped her fist and guided it inward. The momentum of her slash carried the six-inch blade into her trim stomach just below her heart. The blade pointed up.

Her mouth ripped over for a scream. Dartanian's right hand cupped it silent. His left pushed slightly on the hilt. She tumbled off the bed and thumped onto the floor.

He'd given her every chance. But she proved she was a killer, and she paid for it. Dartanian got up and dressed slowly while he looked at Peggy Revere's haunted face. He'd recognized her the moment she stepped into the bar and launched her attempt on his life.

Dartanian took off her platinum wig and stuffed it into his side pocket. Next he removed her pearls and the gaudy gold necklet. He might have been seen with a platinum blond sporting a lot of jewelry, but there was nothing to connect him to this dead redhead.

He shook his head. He didn't like to ICE women, but he was able to do it. She was a killer, and she had to go down. Justice made no exceptions.

Dartanian scanned the room, then looked back at her. It had been a nice try. Her body was distracting. The wig was a perfect fit. But he never forgot a face. As tonight proved, his life often depended on it.

"So long, Peggy," he said. "Don't worry. You won't be lonesome very long."

Lurid pictures of the execution flooded the newspapers the following morning. Despite the hotel's efforts to bury the publicity, every reporter in town had an item. They'd been alerted to the slaying shortly after it happened. By the time the police arrived, the photographers and reporters were waiting for them. They snapped her in the flesh.

It was the kind of tragedy that made good reading over breakfast. The local news programs showed clips of their reporters standing in front of the hotel. Word of the nude woman identified as Peggy Revere saturated the city. She was a sensation.

All the ingredients for a major scandal were present. This was just the kickoff. The sin hounds scented an orgy of murder and lust about to unfold. The media was helped by "unnamed sources" who provided deep background on Peggy Revere and linked her death to the porn massacres staged in New York.

Karen Atwood, the *Action News* reporter who covered Melonie Grand early in the case, had the most detailed story. Dartanian gave her enough leads to stay ahead of the competition for at least a week. He had other conduits in the media, but she was the key figure for this one.

Her well-known Goldilocks curls bounced on camera for the first part of her clip. "This is Karen Atwood at a midtown hotel, scene of a tragic murder that follows closely on the heels of what appears to be a pornography vendetta. Peggy Revere, the popular wife of evangelist Luke Revere, was stabbed to death in a sixth-floor room. Police discovered her naked body shortly after midnight. She had checked into the room under an assumed name. The question before us is this—what was Peggy Revere doing in that hotel room? Why was she killed?"

The next clip came from the studio. Karen

Atwood spoke before a changing backdrop that showed photographs of Peggy Revere clothed and unclothed. Clips of the earlier porn massacres were followed by suggestive promo shots from Melonie's upcoming *Starlet* flick.

After whetting the viewer's appetite, Karen dropped the bomb. "A possible reason for the killing is the rumored existence of an alleged porno film featuring an evangelist and Melonie Grand. Perhaps Peggy was simply in the wrong place at the wrong time, and the killer mistakenly thought she was involved."

Karen paused. She sighed as if she hated to break the news. "*I* have seen the videotape rumored to feature a preacher engaged in pornographic activity. The actress in the X-rated performance is indeed Melonie Grand. However, until expert analysis shows the veracity of the film, I am not at liberty to divulge the identity of the man."

The petite reporter tossed a few more sordid morsels to her audience and closed with a teaser. "Reliable sources in the police sector have informed me that several copies of this tape are about to be released to the media. I'll have an update on the situation as developments occur. Until then, this is Karen Atwood for *Action News*."

Luke Revere switched off the television and stared. "I'm destroyed," he said. "Dead. They're wiping me out. One limb at a time. The deacons are getting slaughtered. Peggy's been *murdered.* I . . . lov . . . I liked having her around. She was good. Better than any of your goddamn deacons, better than any of them . . . *Do you hear me!*"

"Yeah. Ya sound like one of your sheep." Archer was tired. He'd been baby-sitting the shell-shocked preacher all day. As the news bulletins increased in savagery, the preacher seemed to shrink. He was incoherent. Revere balanced self-pity and vengeance on a scale of tears. He raged at the television like it was a living thing.

The two men were locked into the chapel. Revere kept staring at the doors like he was waiting for someone to smash them down. He was ready to bounce off the walls.

Archer waited for the brazen heart of the con man to start pumping again. It would come. Revere was too much of a greedy bastard to give up the church built on American suckerhood without a fight.

Archer wondered what he would do if he was in Revere's position. *The same thing he always did. Walk over it and don't look back.*

Revere stood behind the lectern and switched on the main-gate monitor. He saw a line of cars across the street from the gate. It was 10 o'clock at night, and they were still there. A half-dozen men and one woman sat on the hoods of their cars. A quarter moon glimmered on the chrome trim and the headlights. Cigarette glows came from half of the faces.

The sight of the reporters pushed him off another cliff. "What the fuck are they still doing there? I told you to get rid of them!" Earlier in the afternoon, TV and newspaper reporters latched onto twenty Bible students walking around the interior of the Revere Institute. The students babbled into microphones for ten minutes until Magyar herded them from the gate like stray cows.

From then on, the reporters attacked the gate any time they saw movement inside. When it got dark, Revere sent Magyar and a goon squad of deacons to chase off the reporters.

Archer steepled his fingers to his lips. "This ain't exactly the best time to clue you in, brother."

"*Clue* me in, dammit! Why are those reporters still there?"

"They ain't reporters."

"What?"

"They didn't scare. When Magyar went to roust their asses, not a soul moved. The fuckers got cameras and they clicked shots, but they ain't reporters and they ain't photographers. Guess who they are."

Revere's teeth clicked shut. "Dartanian."

Archer nodded. "What they're doin' is identifying your hard guys. Don't send any more down there."

Revere's brown hair fell over his eyes when his head sank down. He rubbed his temples in an effort to see through the pain.

"Man, you need some salvation. Come on, baby, give yourself a dose of that good ole Sunday morning horse shit."

Revere sat before the lectern, silent as a dead man. If he didn't turn himself around now, it was all over for the Revere empire.

"Fuck it, man," Archer said. "I'm not hanging around, if you can't stand up."

"Satan!" Revere shouted.

"What?"

"That's the way out of this. For a start, anyway. Oh, God, it's perfect! It's perfect." Revere waved his hands the same way he exhorted his audiences. This time it was directed at himself. He was a believer.

"Right. Whatever you say." Archer smiled. Things

would be easier now. He didn't have to think of flight from Dartanian. He didn't have to go out on the road imagining there was a bullet racing behind him. It was cut and dry. They were going to fight. He crossed his arms and took pleasure in the way his biceps pressed against his palms like warm rock.

"We'll beat them," Revere said. "Oh, wait and see, God, it's going to work."

"That's the ticket, baby. We fight. It makes the best sense. This ain't a cop matter, so we just got to worry about Dartanian's crew. We beat them, it's clear riding."

The despair melted. Revere's con-man chatter prophesied a glorious victory for the forces of the righteous—righteous meaning anyone who slaughtered Dartanian's men. He and Archer mapped out the campaign. They had to leave the Institute. When the tape came out, he would be ruined. Unless he took the offensive.

There were more than 300 people staying at the Revere Institute. A third of them were students and the rest were volunteers, administrative people, and deacons. Of the deacons, close to 50 were ready to die. Dartanian wouldn't know who those 50 were until it was too late. The exodus was about to begin. Revere hoped to confuse the men watching with a massive caravan. They couldn't follow everyone.

Once they were on the move, Revere could buy time. If he destroyed Dartanian, he could come out on top. The public would fall for Revere's explanation—if he survived. To do that meant it was time to unleash the dogs. Archer had recruited more men like Magyar. The crusade was ready to break camp.

"Set up the equipment and call those damn reporters back out here. Tell them they've got an exclusive Luke Revere interview concerning those unfortunate killings."

Forty-five minutes later, Revere sent Archer to the gate. He handed a videotape to each reporter that showed up. Excerpts of the tape made it onto the late-evening news broadcasts.

Ten minutes before her *Action News* broadcast at 11:30, Karen Atwood dialed a number and spoke briefly on a tape recording. The recording traveled over two more cutaway phone signals before reaching Dartanian.

He was in his office on the top floor of the ICE tower on Cage Street when a light flashed on his red phone. He clicked the lit button and heard Karen Atwood's voice. She told him about the Revere videotape about to go on the air. She had made a copy for him. It was waiting at the station.

Dartanian smiled. He alreayd had a copy of Revere's tape. One of the "reporters" had been an ICE agent. Still, for appearance's sake he would send an agent down to pick up Karen's tape.

She knew him only as a voice and a number. He was her most often "unimpeachable source" who directed her to the heart of breaking stories. In turn, she provided him with whatever information he requested.

It was a nicc relationship. She called him on an untraceable connection. He spoke to her with an electronically altered voice on another series of relays. The few times she had met him, she had no idea he was her source.

Dartanian watched her broadcast for the highlights of Revere's response to the scandal smoking him out.

"Satan is out to destroy me. He's out to destroy you, and all we've worked for. Why? Because we are winning the fight. Be-cuzzzzz he is worried that you and I are going to beat the devil! That is why he has manufactured lies about me! That is why Satan's agents have murdered dear Peggy. That is why I am talking to you now. We have got to stop this humanist plot against us and all we stand for. You know the media is against God and for abortion. Against God and for evolution. And the media is against me and for Satan. As proof, they are circulating a doctored film that purports to be me and some fallen woman in carnal congress."

Revere's face soured. The thought of sex with a porn star repulsed him. The thought that some good Christians might be led astray by the godless media pained him. The thought that anyone could join forces with the devil and thus condemn themselves to hell appalled him. He ended his short speech with the conclusion that anyone who believed the lies about him was going straight to hell.

"Remember, Satan is out to get me. And you. Let's stick together and find the truth. You, me, and God."

The excerpt ended.

Dartanian shook his head. He'd been called many things, but it was the first time he had ever been referred to as the devil. It was a nice touch. Revere's followers would believe him for the simple reason that he'd long ago conditioned them not to trust the media. The media always lied about evangelists and created exposés, because they were controlled by the devil. So much for his followers.

Revere was sharp enough to evade the police

and any government investigation into his activities. Dartanian was certain of that. There were too many Reveres running loose to make him think otherwise.

All you have to worry about is me, Dartanian thought. The blond headman of ICE looked out the long windows and down at *his* city. He saw men and women walking the streets in safety. He saw the alleys clean of two-legged scavengers. He saw a city full of human beings. The animals had been extinguished. The vision faded with the ringing of the white phone. Below, he saw empty streets where few dared to walk at this hour. The city was a battlefield for Dartanian's small army and the armies of the night.

He caught the phone on the second ring. It was Mick Porter. "The fox is running," he said.

Twelve

The Revere Bible Institute went on alert at 12:03 a.m. High wattage flood lights turned the parking lot into daylight for the hundreds of people boarding the buses. It looked like a military camp cracking the troops for an assault.

Revere stood beside Archer as the giant deacon selected passengers at random for each bus. He mixed deacons with students and scattered rougher-looking men among each batch. It was done in full view of the watchers just outside the gate. Dartanian's men could see for themselves the grouping of innocents with the guilty. That was to Revere's advantage. He and Archer had figured Dartanian's major weakness. The man wouldn't slaughter innocents. If all of Revere's followers took off at once, the buses would be safe from immediate attack.

In his brown suit, Revere looked like he was ready to do some serious preaching. His eyes glowed with Ministry fire. His hair was waxed into place. He was freshly shaven. This was not the man who sat dejectly in his chapel a short time ago. This was a man with a plan. This was one of God's generals leading a battalion of Christian soldiers.

In less than 10 minutes, the touring buses were boarded. They used the entire fleet although eight would have been enough for the crusade. Three of the buses were Revere's flagships, former Diamond-T's converted into luxury vehicles. Their raised roofs and comfort compartments served as home for Revere's elite on the crusades. Tonight they carried several coed Bible students, volunteer workers, and normal deacons who looked forward to this chance to serve God. Like Revere's rough boys, the fighting deacons, they were sprinkled among each bus. They were eager. Revere's pep talk still rang in their ears. Soon they could be in heaven.

Revere boarded one of the silver touring buses. He sat next to a 19-year-old girl who flushed and bit her lower lip. She felt like an angel had sat next to her.

"This is my first crusade," she said. "It's so exciting."

"It's something you'll never forget, child." He beamed a paternal guardian smile at her. He'd told her and the other students they were going on a minicrusade to experience the Lord's work firsthand. He looked at the black-haired teenager sitting beside him. Such a lovely decoy, he thought.

The buses moved out.

Revere screamed. He jumped from his seat and ran to the front of the bus. "No! Dammit, no!" He stared at the procession of buses ahead of him. They shook and waddled and flapped toward the front gate.

His bus moved forward. The left side collapsed. Revere gripped the pole behind the driver. "That sonofabitch thinks of everything!"

"Sorry," the driver said. He had never seen Revere like this before. It shook him. God's right-hand man wasn't supposed to swear. "It's not my fault," he said when Revere's knuckles turned white and another stream of curses poured from his half-closed mouth.

Buses pulled out of the procession like wounded soldiers falling at the wayside. One by one, the drivers realized the tires on one side of their buses were flat. Pressure from the rolling buses squeezed out the last gasps of air from the shredded rubber.

Revere jumped from the bus. He raced around the parking lot looking for Archer. He shouted inside each bus for him, darting like a mad dog until he found him. Archer grabbed his arm and led him away from a pack of students staring at him in the parking lot.

"How did he do it?" Revere asked. "How the fuck did they get in here without anyone seeing them?" He rocked on his feet, tapping out the panic. His head bobbed, and his hands clenched and unclenched. He'd been short-circuited.

"He did it, man," Archer said. "Don't worry about how. Just deal with it. Come on, tough it up. Everybody's looking."

Revere straightened his shoulders. "Deal with it," he repeated.

"Right. Let's get you inside your Diamond-T. Do a few lines of C and get your head straight. See, that bus is untouched, man. They didn't get them all." Deacon Archer guided Revere to the intact green Diamond-T bus. He went inside first and shouted at the startled passengers in the front compartment. "Out! Everybody outside. We gotta regroup."

Another stream of passengers joined the confusion in the parking lot. Archer came out of the Diamond-T a minute later. He found Magyar in a group of deacons. "Kill those fucking lights," Archer said.

Twenty minutes later, three buses headed for the gate in the darkness. Of the entire fleet, all that was road-worthy were one Diamond-T, a silver tour bus, and an equipment bus. Archer's personal recruits and the deacons dominated the entourage, although he was sure to include some of the innocents on each bus.

Revere was calm by the time they rolled through the gate. Beside him in the personal compartment was the black-haired girl. He'd invited her to share some prayers. She'd been a bit afraid at first, after witnessing his outburst. But she knew great men carried great burdens. It was her duty to help him through the rough time.

Six cars fell in line behind the buses. They made no effort to disguise the surveillance. Revere was aware of the tail, but he wasn't worried. Archer had a way to take care of them.

Thank God for Archer, he thought. He turned to the pretty girl beside him. Thank God for her. She was just what he needed.

Val Wagner tailed the Diamond-T when the buses split up at Tarrytown. A Homer transmitter attached to the undercarriage of the bus was set to the frequency of the radio pickup in her black Chrysler Imperial.

The wrecking crew had planted Homer transmitters on the three intact buses. Two ICE vehicles were locked onto each one. Sin Simara drove backup for Val in a Datsun 280-Z.

Val rolled down the driver's window to let the night air rush in and keep her alert. It looked like it was going to be a long drive. The Diamond-T played a cat-and-mouse game on I-87 North. At the last minute, the huge green bus would cut over to the exit. Then it would either follow a side road or jump over the crossroad and roar back onto I-87.

She chased it through Tuxedo Park, Highland Mills, and then found herself winding over desolate narrow roads with rows of pine standing guard on both sides. The driver of the Diamond-T hurtled around the curves like a maniac. At times she could hear the groaning engine of the bus. It was crying for mercy, but the driver kept up the hurtling pace.

It drifted in and out of sight. Val didn't worry about losing it. The Homer system was an excellent tracking device. And on top of having Sin Simara behind her, Dartanian had Revere's probable destination worked out.

To break the monotony of the drive, Val maintained radio contact with Simara. She knew that he talked for her benefit. He liked the silence.

"This is the place," Archer said. The driver nodded. Just north of Wallkill, he hit the brakes. Archer, Magyar, and four more bikers threw down the ramp at the rear of the bus. They rolled their Harley's down the ramp and split up on each side of the road. Their black jackets matched the machines as they waited in the woods.

Archer straddled his Harley like a modern-day cowboy. Instead of a Winchester laying across the metal horse's neck, he had a KG9. Magyar was on the other side of the road about seventy yards up.

"It's coming!" Archer shouted.

The powerful roar of the Chrysler reached them just before it came into sight. By then, the KG9's were lifted. Everyone of them had been fixed. Instead of the legal pistols they had once been, they were fully automatic machine pistols.

"Do it!" Archer shouted.

They stood on their iron horses and strafed the windshield. 96 rounds of 9mm slugs poured into the glass. "Fuck," he said when he saw that it was bulletproof. Even so, the pock marks destroyed the driver's vision.

The Chrysler veered all over the road. It nipped a row of pines on Archer's side before straightening out. But the road curved. If the car made it past the curve, Magyar was there to deal with it. Beyond that was a clearing where they could finish it off.

Archer reclipped the KG9. He kicked the Harley onto the road and led the two other bikers after the Chrysler. He heard three more clips blast up ahead. Tires screeched. Six bikes bore down on the black car as it careened over the rough brush into the clearing.

Val Wagner had managed to roll up the driver's window after the first volley of automatic fire. She managed to keep the car steady. The windshield was a crumbled mess from the machine gun punching. If they'd shot her from the side. . . .

By the time she managed to find a clear spot on the base of the windshield, she was hit again. She turned off into a field she had caught in her last brief glimpse of the road. She knew they expected it. It was better than smashing into the trees or stopping in the middle of the road to get picked apart.

Her head smashed into the roof of the car, then snapped back until she heard the cartilage in her neck creak. The Chrysler bumped and dug its way over the field. Val waited until she reached a reasonably level patch of high-forest grass. She cranked the wheel all the way to the left and spun the car just as the growling bikes reached her.

The back end crunched into a bike. She heard a scream. Then she heard round after round of slugs pour into the car. She managed to empty one clip of her Ingram M11 through the gunport as she wheeled the car in a dirt-spitting circle.

"It's a bitch!" Magyar shouted. "It's just a bitch, and she's kicking our ass. Kill her." He chopped the driver's side of the car with a clip.

Val rode it out to the end. She could no longer see. She could just hear them gunning her down. It was only a matter of time before they broke through. She slammed the car in reverse and heard another scream. The crunched bike served as traction when she pushed the gear lever forward. The big Chrysler hopped forward, spinning and dancing like a bull among matadors.

It crashed head-on into a fat oak. A thick limb elbowed through the torn windshield and cracked her forehead. Val slumped behind the wheel.

Archer looked at the wrecked Chrysler. He glanced at three dead bikers. "Make sure," he said to Magyar. He drove back to the road with the remaining biker.

Magyar pried the driver's door open. He dragged Val out of the seat and threw her down on the dirt. His left hand knotted her hair and lifted her neck off the ground. His right hand unsnapped a knife with a curved two-edged blade. He brought the knife over his left shoulder for a downward throat slash with the razor-sharp curve.

Whooosh!

Dull black metal sliced the air. The back of

Magyar's hand sprouted a steel shooting star as his knife descended. The knife dropped. Magyar grunted and plucked the shuriken out of his hand. Blood jumped from the ripped skin.

He crouched low to the ground. Then he saw the thin shape coming at him. The Japanese man was silent as he crossed the ground. Magyar laughed when he saw the size of his attacker. He stood and raised his bloody hand over his head to use as a club. The gory fist swooped for the Japanese man's skull.

Magyar, who never bothered to feel pain, found out what he'd been missing all these years. His fist went down but stopped a fraction of an inch from his small attacker. At that moment, there was a loud snap. His shattered forearm exploded. Bone shards jabbed through his skin. The arm looked like it had been sawed in half.

He screamed. He looked at the Japanese man with a pain-soaked face as if to say, *Now look what you've done.* Magyar fell forward, somehow thinking that if he made it to the ground the pain would stop.

Before he touched the earth, an even greater pain grabbed him. Ice-pick toes whipped through his neck and curved through his jaw. The lower part of his head was pulverized, moving, exploding, blasting up into his brain until a growing blackness promised the pain would end soon. By the time he thudded onto the dirt, the pain was gone along with the life of the creature that had been Magyar. He laid there like a dead bear.

Simara looked at Val, then raced over the grassy clearing. He kept close to the dark, closely bunched trees.

"Magyar!" Archer's voice sailed through the clearing. "Come on!" He called his name again. It was weaker this time, as if he'd suddenly realized something horrible was coming his way.

A shuriken whizzed by his ear when he turned his bike in a half circle. If instinct hadn't prodded the move, his head would have been split. "Go!" he shouted. The two bikers whipped down the road, headlights off and heads down.

The private compartment inside the speeding Diamond-T bus resembled a whorehouse in spite of the religious totems. Blond wood paneling sealed all four walls. Red leather couches were bolted to the floor, surrounding a bar on three sides. Crosses faced each other from the front and back walls.

A red satin bedroom took up a third of the rolling suite. Videotapes were scattered all over the soft scarlet carpet. It looked like Hugh Hefner's playroom, and the effect wasn't lost on the black-haired girl who sat next to Revere. She'd kicked her feet up on the low bar table in front of her. Like master, like follower.

Revere sat by a tinted four-foot window. His leonine head rolled with the motion of the bus. The dark countryside was soothing to the preacher. Ever since they'd been on the road, he'd calmed down.

Denise Courtland was no longer afraid of Luke Revere. She had sipped sherry with him, talked of God's work, and found out that beneath all the charisma he was really a nice, ordinary man. He was a gentle, caring sort who really understood her problems.

Luke Revere had picked her as a traveling companion. It was one of the high points in her life. *Wait until she told the girls.*

The handsome preacher went right on charming her until Deacon Archer came back. The bus stopped. There was a commotion at the rear. Angry voices carried through the night. She went to the window and peered out. Archer, another man, and Luke Revere stood off the road. Revere's hands waved up and down. He screamed just like he did back in the parking lot at the Institute.

The argument continued on the bus. Archer and Revere shouted all the way to the compartment. She listened at the door and pretended not to notice anything wrong when Revere stormed inside. The preacher screamed, "Let's hope the others do better!" He slammed the door in Archer's face. He leaned against the door and seemed to melt. His tall posture collapsed, and he actually began to slide down. His face was sweating and his eyes were glassy.

The head turned slowly toward her. He seemed startled to see her there.

She was here all along. Melonie Grand was sitting next to him. How foolish of him not to realize it until now. It was probably the black hair, but the more he talked to her the better her hair got. It changed to yellow, bright and curly, falling down her shoulders.

Luke Revere laughed. It was just like old times. He dropped his arm around her and pulled her close. She acted shy. He brought out some coke for the two of them and laid it out on the table, but she pretended she didn't do coke.

Melonie was such a kick. Too bad she caused all that trouble. The sassy bitch was out to ruin him.

"Have some," he said.

"Look, I know you're under a lot of pressure—"

"Take it!" He pushed her head down to the table. The white powder smeared all over her face. Then she had the nerve to turn her hair black and pretend she wasn't Melonie. She screamed. He hit her. She grew quiet and reasonable. He hit her again to make sure she stayed that way.

She crouched in the curved pocket of the red leather couch.

Luke Revere sidled over to her. He kissed her neck. She slid away. Her blouse tore in his hand. He laughed and ripped it all the way. Then he yanked the bra down. "It's so good to be together again," he said. She squirmed in his hands. "Stop it!" Her breasts bobbled in his hands. "Pull yourself together!" He kicked off his clothes.

Melonie cried. *What an actress!* She was such a fake. She felt good though, all that creamy flesh in his hands again. It was so much better than that damn tape. She was real now. She wasn't on the screen. She was under him, bucking, giving it to him, screaming, *what an actress!*

"I missed you so much," he said. "I've been waiting for this so long, uhhh, so damn long. Here you go!" He fell on top of her and crushed her with a violent orgasm.

She shook her head from side to side.

"You've got to be quiet about all this," he said. "Promise you'll be quiet."

She nodded. He helped her. His hands clasped around her neck. They squeezed and pushed. Her head slid over the edge of the leather couch. He bent it back until it cracked. Revere left her there.

He mixed a drink and went back to his vigil by the window. He was still sitting there calmly when Archer stepped into the compartment.

"Oh man, you've done it again! Oh, fuck, man, no, *I don't believe it!* The worst possible time."

"What's eating you?" Revere said. "*I* got Melonie, didn't I? I did what you couldn't."

Archer stared at him like he'd done something wrong. Revere shook his head. Sometimes Archer didn't understand things too well.

But then Revere saw what was bothering him. The girl's hair had turned black again. Dammit! This had to stop. "Get rid of her," he said. *That bitch Melonie was out of control.*

Thirteen

Mick Porter's Country Squire swallowed the road with quiet hunger. The reconditioned battle wagon was a perfect fit for Mick. It was sturdy and large and faster than it looked. If he had to pour on the juice, the Country Squire could roar.

The stocky ICE agent kept his eye on the tail lights of Ed Cameron's Dodge Charger. Ed had held the lead ever since their bus picked up Route 9 North outside of Tarrytown. Revere's tour bus led them through Wappingers Falls, Poughkeepsie, and turned off Route 9 at Hyde Park.

Now it was cruising east toward Salt Point. It fit in with Dartanian's scenario. The blond ICE leader had put himself in Revere's place. He and Mick spent hours with Reverend Soames evaluating Revere's present state of mind. They had to nail down his escape sites.

Where would Revere go if he were forced to leave the Institute? Dartanian had asked.

It would never happen, Soames had answered. Revere wouldn't leave his multimillion-dollar haven.

But if he had to leave, Dartanian had persisted, what was the most likely destination?

Soames gave three sites. Dartanian selected the one in Duchess County as Revere's first choice. The ICE teams were ready to assault the preacher's "Heaven on Earth" retreat south of Millbrook. If it turned out to be another site, the ICE force would find it. One way or another, Revere's judgment day was at hand.

The gentle rocking of the Country Squire gave way to periodic jolts. They were riding into rougher country. Mick's eyes followed the white line. His mind clicked into that special calm. He was alert but detached. Instinct had taken over.

A quick summer shower pelted the windshield for three minutes. Fresh forest breezes whirled into the wagon. It smelled of hunting and camping. Too bad he was on a different kind of hunt.

Mick's eyes darted to the rear-view mirror. A peripheral motion had just flashed across the mirror. He couldn't tell if it was night shadows from the wooded hills or if something actually moved behind him.

He tried catching the reflection a few more times, but it always seemed that whenever he looked the movement ended. A chill rushed across the back of his neck. What the hell, he thought. He killed the headlights of the battle wagon. His foot popped off the accelerator, taking the Country Squire down to a 40 mile an hour crawl.

Moonlight bounced from chrome behind him. His mirror held a pair of black cars swooping down on him. He glanced out the window for a clearer view and saw a third dark car behind them.

"We're not alone," Mick radioed to Ed Cameron. "I got three hawks on my tail. I'm gonna take 'em." Mick gassed the wagon. The speedometer whacked up to 90 mph. He flew over a stretch of farm-dotted road looking for a relatively deserted area. He didn't want to shoot up any Farmer John who happened to be in the way.

That's it! He braked the wagon the instant he saw the smoked ruins of a barn alongside the road. Mick spun the wheel to the left and screeched a one-eighty on the tar. He hopped the wagon off the road and spun it once more in a patch of high grass. The Country Squire came to a stop facing the road, hidden by the barn. Mick could see the triad coming for him through the wrecked slats of the barn. It was perfect. He was acres away from the closest farmhouse.

"Burnt out barn," Mick radioed. "It'll be on your right."

He waited for Revere's men. They'd been totally unexpected. Most of the hard guys were on the buses. ICE held a watch over the Institute. These cars must have come from other Revere hideouts. Wherever they came from, they weren't going back.

For a moment, Mick thought it might just be a pack of hill boys raising hell on the roads. That thought died when the first black car whipped by. He saw a lot of killing hardware hanging out the windows.

The lead car screeched to a stop. The other two prowled toward him. Damn! They had seen his maneuver. It was party time. Mick stomped the accelerator. The wagon jacked toward the creeping pairs of cars. He flicked the Thompson switch and spun the steering wheel on a slow arc to the right. Mick strafed both vehicles, ducked, and raced the wagon around the barn.

The third car slammed him from the back. Mick bounced like a rag doll in the front seat and gripped the wheel. He managed to straighten it out while submachine guns barked at his back. Wood splintered on his right. One of the strafed cars burst through the barn and rocked into the wagon. Both cars smacked him again, pinching him, tilting him on two wheels.

They were pushing him over. He would be dead when that happened, trapped inside a metal turtle on its back. Mick bailed out. Fire snaked over his left shoulder. Bullets ripped through his flapping khaki shirt. He dove into the high grass and ate dirt. Mick's elbows marched double time, raw and bleeding, propelling him out of the immediate line of fire. He rolled, somersaulted, and swam through the field.

He couldn't tell how many there were, but they emptied a few hundred rounds into the high grass. He dug his way about 30 yards from the action. His head was so close to the ground he could hear their footfalls travel through the earth. That sound was followed by the whispering of tall grass as it was pushed aside by the searchers.

Anytime now, Ed, he thought. *Join the party.* Mick looked up at the stars. He cut down his breathing to let the air silently seep in and out of his mouth. Mick became part of the environment, a rocky shape molded to the earth, shielded by high grass.

Voices grew louder. They were closer. He held the trigger of the Ingram M10 balanced on his chest. His heels dug into the dirt. The grass in front of him rippled.

Closer, closer. Three of them were silhouetted in the starlight. They had night gear. They had a lot of numbers on their side.

One man stepped on Mick's foot. He screamed and jumped back like something bit him.

Mick squeezed the trigger. He popped up like a

jack-in-the-box and sprayed the three men with fifteen rounds. Before they fell dead to the ground, he curled and dove back into the grass, rolling away from the fire he'd drawn.

Another Ingram opened up from the road. Screams and 9mm Parabellum whines chorused in the night. Ed Cameron had come on in ICE fashion, totally quiet until it was killing time.

Mick mowed the grass in front of him with fifteen more rounds and slapped another clip in the Ingram. Farm dogs bayed in the distance. He could picture the farmers grabbing shotguns in case the fireworks came their way.

Whispering grass sounded again. This time it was louder than before. The ambushers were stampeding away. Mick knelt in the grass and blasted the panicked amateurs before they had a chance to regroup and get lucky.

Ed Cameron cut down two men who managed to reach the imagined safety of their cars. The two ICE agents then scoured the field for survivors. Only three minutes had passed since the first shots were fired. In that time, Hell welcomed a new pack of recruits.

Fourteen

Millbrook, New York, was a small provincial town in Duchess County that once served as home for Timothy Leary. Aside from Gordon Liddy's raid on the acid guru's estate in the Sixties, nothing much happened in the region.

The towns around Millbrook were small. The country was pretty. There was plenty of space to get away from it all. Luke Revere quietly bought property in Millbrook, nearby Washington Hollow, and hundreds of wilderness acres midway between the hollow and Nuclear Lake.

Just as Walt Disney created his Disneyland fantasy for middle America to visit, Luke Revere created "Heaven on Earth" as a showcase for his followers. It was his very own village. He designed it to appeal to the fundamentalists' nostalgia for the good old days. Revere's Ministry millions carved paradise out of the wilderness acres.

In the center of the private village was a white wooden church with a bell tower. Twenty stained-glass windows slivered the long sides of the church. Forty yards south of the church was a tremendous gazebo. Ministry choir groups often sang under the roof of the open-aired hexagon for the Bible students and volunteers going through indoctrination.

White colonial homes served as dormitories and meeting halls. There was an old-fashioned general store and a religious shop on Heaven's Main Street. Close to the woods was a stable of horses. It was the good life.

At four in the morning, Revere's three buses had converged on Millbrook. They formed a caravan on the way south through Washington Hollow and reached Heaven on Earth just as the first birds of morning broke into song.

Revere was in control of himself. Coke and amphetamines perked him up with the "power." He was in his element. He had to speak to the people. Archer took over security for the camp and spread his deacons throughout the buildings.

There were 42 people who actually thought they were on the first leg of a Ministry Crusade. Despite their lack of sleep and the uncomfortable bus ride, they were in fine spirits.

Luke Revere had invited them all to a dawn service. No one thought of refusing. That kind of action was selfish and Satan-inspired. Besides, there was something about Revere's bodyguards that unnerved them.

Five of them raced through Heaven on huge motorcycles. They had fearsome expressions, although none of them actually bothered to "see" the parishioners. They looked through them as they herded them toward the church.

The parishioners were uneasy, and though the one called Deacon Archer was the scariest of them all, they were glad he was there. He kept the other brutes under control. The parishioners smiled at the bikers and filed inside the church. After all, everyone in Heaven was a good Christian, even the ones in black leather.

While a crew of deacons set up the video cameras in the church, Luke Revere met with Archer outside. Just seeing the tall man was reassuring. He had a look on his face that Revere had never quite seen before. Archer was geared for battle. His eyes darted around the homey village, and though he talked with Revere, his mind was elsewhere.

"It's beautiful," Revere said. "We'll film this and get it out to the faithful. Then we'll hit and run, staying one step ahead of those bastards."

"Uh-huh," Archer said.

Revere caught the mocking tone in the biker's voice. "You're the one who said we're ahead of 'em. We shook the tails long before Millbrook." The preacher waved his hands, "You said we could count on being clear of them."

Archer folded his hands over his biceps. He glared at the preacher. "What I said ain't always what is. Don't count on nothin'."

"What's wrong? Dammit, you're growing soft!"

"Three cars full of deacons are supposed to be here by now. Maybe the tails on the last two buses dropped. Maybe our boys in the cars dropped."

Revere laughed. "Don't conjure up trouble." He glanced at the church, sensing that the congregation was getting restless. "Look around you, Archer. We're in Heaven. Listen to the birds, feel the breeze. It's safe as milk."

Archer nodded. He took in the pastoral landscape. Three bikes were parked outside the church. Two more patrolled the grounds. Deacons strolled inside the gates of Heaven, marching close to the razor-wired fence. The bits of razor were honed so sharply that a man could cut himself without knowing it and bleed to death 10 minutes later.

"You're right," Archer said. "It feels great here. But that's the problem. Traps are supposed to feel great."

Revere laughed. It was funny how their roles changed. First Archer talked him out of panic and now he stood there picking out ghosts in the shadows. "I gotta go speak to my people," he said.

"Give 'em hell," Archer said. "And make sure you got your gun, man."

Revere patted the bulge beneath his brightly colored robes.

"Heavenly," Archer said.

A minute later, Revere stormed the stage. He raised his hands upward. The flowing robes shimmered under the bright video lights. The audience jumped to their feet and clapped. Two rows of deacons stood in front of the stage, facing the crowd. They joined the furor and shouted, "Praise God," "God Bless," and "Hallelujah!"

The deacons wore deep red cassocks that covered them from neck to toe. Beneath the white satin cloaks that fell to their waists were holstered KG9s—all of them fixed for full automatic fire.

In the pandemonium, Revere slid his machine pistol into the shelf of the wooden pulpit on center stage. His left hand shot to the ceiling. The crowd quieted down. There were nearly a score of Bible students—wide-eyed girls under Revere's spell, young men headed for a life of suffocating brain death in the Ministry—and an equal number of older male and female volunteers. Every member of the congregation stared at the man on stage who seemed to grow in stature when his eyes burned with the fire.

"We shall vanquish the enemy!" Revere shouted. *"I swear to you and to God above that I will win!"* He scanned the faces. Their eyes were rapt, their minds begging for a new program to follow.

"As you know," he continued in a soft voice of reason, "the Ministry has fought particularly hard against *pornnnn-og-rapheeeeee.* And we were winning, weren't we?"

A chorus of "Amen" and "Praise God" filled the church.

Revere nodded. "That is why Satan's agents have spread lies about me. That is why Satan's agents have manufactured a phony film about me and a harlot. My enemies attack me because they are worried that God's Christian soldiers are winning the fight. Oh, they'll make it reasonable, and they'll try to sow doubt in your minds, but don't give in to Satan! Not now! Not after we've come this far! Stick together in prayer and we shall defeat them! Luke Revere does not run away from satan!"

Although the congregation was small, they made up for it with shouts, falling into a baying that resembled a mass speaking in tongues.

"Like Jesus before me I will go into the wilderness for 40 days to listen to my soul and to listen to God, and when I come back, I shall be proven innocent of the slanderous charges heaped upon me. I will lead the Ministry in it's glorious fight against the devil and all his minions! *And it starts right here in Heaven on Earth. This will be the launch pad into heaven above. From here I shall prevail against the hounds of Satan!"*

A black Harley rumbled into the back of the church. It thundered up the steps and sailed into the air at the top. Every head turned to see a black-clad rider crouching over the handlebars.

The biker gunned the Harley down the center aisle. He leaned into a controlled skid at the front of the church and whipped the bike past the right front pews.

"What the hell?" Revere's voice boomed through the microphone. He stared at the man in the black visored helmet. He noticed the weapons crisscrossing the biker's chest now that he was still for a moment.

The man in black fired a machine pistol burst four feet above the pews. "Everybody out!" The pistol waved them back.

The women screamed. The men shouted. In a panicked herd, they milled to the back of the church. They poured out of the rear exit like sand through an hourglass.

"What is it?" Revere shouted. "Are we under attack?"

The biker looked at Revere. He saw deacons reach for their guns and stare at the church doors. They expected an army to storm in.

"Answer me!" Revere shouted. "I said, are we under attack!"

"Damn right," the biker said. He pushed the black visored helmet over his head to show blond hair and a killing smile. Dartanian gunned the Harley past the deacons. The Skorpion M61 spit out a clip of 7.65mm stings. The first row of deacons crumpled.

One second after the Skorpion's chatter, the stained-glass windows burst into shards and jangled to the church floor. Smoke and tear gas cannisters smashed through half the windows.

Revere was stunned. He looked at the disorganized deacons thrashing into each other. Smoke and gas billowed around them in a black cloud.

Dartanian charged his Harley at the deacons in front of the stage.

The preacher grabbed the KG9 and fired it through the wooden pulpit. 9mm slugs blasted the cluster of deacons in front of Dartanian. An older deacon with weeds of gray hair spun as he fell. His last realization was that Revere had shot him in the back in an attempt to hit the blond man.

Gunfire erupted from every corner of the village. Deacons emptied their weapons and ran for the church exits. Machine gun teeth chewed them in half. ICE agents had sealed every exit. There was no escape. In less than a minute, 24 deacons lay dead or dying on the church floor. They were fierce when it came to ambushing porn stars. When real soldiers brought the war to them, they fell apart.

Revere saw Dartanian hop onto the stage. The preacher fled through a side door to the rectory and slammed it behind him.

Dartanian booted the door off its hinges. It smacked flat on the stone floor like a drawbridge leading into the king's castle. The ICE headman charged in with a freshly clipped Skorpion. He caught Revere just as the preacher reached for the far door of the rectory. Dartanian smashed his face into the wooden door before Revere could turn the knob. He circled his iron fingers around the preacher's neck.

Revere turned. He kicked and punched in a blur of unfocused fury. But nothing could break Dartanian's death grip on his throat. Revere's maniac face burst into red blotches. He turned to his left. The choking man clawed at the door.

"It's worse out there," Dartanian said. The sound of battle encircled them. The entire village was under siege—from inside where Dartanian's men had lain hidden all night, and from outside where ICE teams closed off Heaven on Earth from the rest of the world.

"Ohhhh," Revere grunted. He calmed down. His head nodded. The guise of acceptance lasted three seconds. Revere attacked with his fists. The strong blows bounced off Dartanian's granite shoulders with no effect. Dartanian squeezed up on Revere's neck. He tossed him back into the center of the room. The disheveled preacher slid along an eggshell-white wall.

Smoke and gas crept into the connecting room from the church. Dartanian cut him off from the rectory door on the other side.

Fear choked his breath. "What do you want?" he gasped. "We can deal."

Dartanian's eyes showed no emotion. The cold blue ICE gaze held steady on the squirming man. "I want the names and locations of your hit teams for a start."

The preacher's hands inched along the wall behind him as he moved away from fat tongues of smoke heading toward him. "I'm *ruined* without them!" Revere protested. "They're keeping me alive. They'll come after you unless I call 'em off. It gives me something to bargain with."

"I'm what's keeping you alive at the moment," Dartanian said. "Talk! Come on, this is your chance to walk away."

Revere's crazy eyes sparkled. He gave up names and hideouts scattered throughout New York. Pride toughened his voice. He could tell Dartanian was impressed by the great number of hit teams on call.

"Is that all of them?" Dartanian asked.

Revere sighed. "Uhhuh," he said. He relaxed against the wall.

Dartanian aimed the Skorpion machine pistol at his chest.

"But you said I had a chance to walk—"

"Walk. Run. It's your choice. Either way, it's not much of a chance."

In that last fear-soaked moment, Revere knew that Dartanian was *dead* serious. He took a half step . . .

Phyyt-phyyt-phyyt. Dartanian stung him with a clip of three-round bursts. Revere's robe-draped body shuddered in a death fit. Each 7.65mm burst whacked him against the wall. Revere toppled sideways to the floor. Behind him the blood-splotched wall looked like it had been spray-painted with graffitti. *ICE was here.*

Deacon Archer stepped out of the village general store with a pack of cigarettes when hell came to heaven. He'd never seen or even imagined anything like it before. The Diamond-T bus chugged away from the church with a full load of fundamentalists. It crumpled the iron gate at full speed.

Two men in green camouflage gear who'd supervised the embarkment were joined by a running squad of similarly clad men. They raced alongside the church with Armalite AR-18s. In two seconds, the Armalites bashed rifle grenades through the stained-glass windows. The men dropped to the ground and dug in.

Inside. The attack came from inside! Archer saw several sentry deacons lying dead over the razor wire that capped the fencing. Silenced weapons or unarmed combat had taken them out without a peep. Their bodies had been thrown on the wire as bridges for outside troops.

Now that the attack had begun, there was no need for silence. Metal rain poured into every inch of the village from loud assault rifles. Only seconds had passed, and the private heaven was caving in.

It took Archer a few more seconds to pinpoint where the main assault came from. Then he saw the flare of barrel flashes from under the gazebo. Smack in the center of the village, the gazebo offered clear shots at nearly every target. The slats of the gazebo's foundation popped onto the green grass, kicked out by the eight-man sniper team inside. After their first volleys, they charged out into the open.

The agents fired Armalites, Uzis, and Galils on the run. They blasted four deacons off their feet. The deacons had been shooting their KG9's aimlessly.

Deacon Archer was stunned by the beauty of the attack. The lean ex-Marine stood open-mouthed. This elite force had rescued every potential hostage, wrecked the churchful of deacons, and breached the iron gates—all in a matter of seconds. The main battle was already over. It was mop-up time. The instinctive part of Archer's mind took over and threw him down face first on the general store's porch. Walls of glass blew inward from a stitch of machine-gun fire. A hundred tiny shards sprinkled down on his skin.

Archer knew he could get away. The Harley was only three strides away from him. The wooded acres surrounding the village square offered plenty of room to hide. No one would catch him on the Harley.

But Deacon Archer couldn't run. Magyar was dead. He owed him. He also owed Dartanian, and before he could leave, he had to pay him back. The splendidly muscled biker wrestled the Harley upright. He jump-started the iron horse and roared away as another volley of automatic fire rained on the general store. He circled back toward the gazebo and fired a clip of 9mm Parabellum slugs at the previous occupants.

Blood scratches sprouted over his body as the Harley roared over the grass. His black tank top offered no protection from the bits of glass grinding into his skin with each bump. Return fire whipped past his ears. He crouched low to the handlebars and veered toward the woods to reload his machine pistol. He felt like Custer at the Little Big Horn. All of his troops were falling, slaughtered by an unstoppable army. The invaders had been outnumbered almost four-to-one less than a minute ago.

Now there seemed to be hardly any of Revere's men moving along with Archer. He charged into a brush-laden line of oaks. The whipping branches added more cuts to his arms and face. It didn't bother him. Bleeding was second nature in battle. He jammed a 32-round clip into the machine pistol. He wheeled the Harley around and searched for Dartanian.

Tim Reed screeched back into the village with the green Diamond-T after dropping the passengers in the safety of the woods. He rolled slowly past the church. A half-dozen ICE agents swarmed into the bus. Armalite AR-18s spit fire out of the side windows as Reed circled the inside of the village.

Mick Porter stood up in the bell tower, sniping

two wild-looking bearded bikers with a silenced CAR15 rifle. Sin Simara stalked the woods in search of any survivors on the slim chance they escaped the ICE assault.

Dartanian's blond hair and distinctive black war togs kept him from drawing ICE fire while he gunned the Harley chopper over the battleground. Archer hadn't turned up among the bodies. He was out there somewhere. Of them all, Archer was the most dangerous.

He thundered the bike over a grassy hill at the edge of the village clearing. His left hand held the bike, his right the Skorpion. The bike tires chewed up the slanted earth. It was like holding onto a bucking bronco.

Dartanian made one full circuit of the village before Archer screamed out of the trees. His angry Harley grumbled after Dartanian from the back. The blond headman sensed a stream of bullets coming his way. He hugged the hot metal with his head down. Dartanian slapped the Skorpion against his ribs and squeezed off 10 rounds at his ambusher. Archer turned away.

The two bikers wheeled in opposite directions. They turned and faced each other. Deacon Archer's KG9 rattled off the rest of his clip at the same time that Dartanian emptied the Skorpion. Both bikers moved too fast and too crazy for the slugs to find flesh.

Archer stopped to throw in another clip. Dartanian dropped the Skorpion to the ground and gunned the Harley. Rocket-breath exhaust scorched the air while the iron horse dug a trench through the grass. Archer saw there wasn't a spare second to arm the KG9. He grasped the handlebars with both hands and returned the charge.

The Harleys spiked each other head-on in a neck-snapping groan of metal and motor. Dartanian's left leg sizzled on the exhaust when the colliding bikes whipped into a side-by-side position. Archer's face smacked onto the speedometer. He came up with cracked teeth and a blood-stained grin.

"Now!" Archer spat out. The brawny giant reached for Dartanian, expecting to pluck him in the air. Dartanian caught the massive man's wrist with his left. He slapped the fingers with a short palm-heel strike. At the moment of contact, he pushed upward and cracked every finger until it bent backward.

Archer screamed in rage and pain. His body propelled itself with a mind of its own. The giant's good hand thumped Dartanian's chest and knocked him from the wreckage of the bikes. Archer pinned Dartanian's back to the ground. The deacon kneed him in the groin. His huge fist blurred past Dartanian's head and smacked the ground.

The weight crushed Dartanian. Unless he broke the hold, Archer could land the one punch he needed. Dartanian's fists arced like the claws of a lobster. They swooped way out and then fired into Archer's massive body just below his underarms. Archer roared from the cracked cartilage. He fell off, but on his way down he elbowed Dartanian in the face.

Dartanian rolled to his left to get balance. Then he hook-kicked his right foot into Archer's spine.

"Uhhhhh!" Archer's body jerked as though a meat hook had trashed his back. He crawled away.

The fighters forced their battered bodies to stand. Both were bleeding and bruised. Dartanian stepped forward and surprised the big man. Archer wasn't used to being charged. His size always prevented that in the past.

Dartanian landed a front snap kick to his chest. It was like kicking rock. Archer fired back a roundhouse kick to Dartanian's ribs. He followed through with an overhand punch to Dartanian's temple.

The blond warrior dropped to the ground. His left foot swept behind Archer's right ankle. A millesecond later Dartanian pistoned his right foot into Archer's knee. It broke. Archer fell like an oak. He bellowed in agony. His wasted body flopped around as though it were shot through with electricity.

Dartanian hovered above him. He pinned Archer's right shoulder to the ground. He thought of the names Revere had given him. Now was a good time to check it out.

"Tell me who else is working for you."

Archer couldn't talk. The pain locked his teeth. Sweat and blood ran down his face. His head shook from left to right.

"Tell me," Dartanain commanded. "You might save some innocent lives."

Archer hissed through clenched teeth. "Fuck 'em!"

Dartanian pistoned three kill techniques to Archer's body in a half second. His right fist cracked the skull. His left spear hand ripped into the throat. His right fist imploded Archer's heart.

The giant was dead.

Epilogue

The camera hit Karen Atwood for a close-up of the pained face beneath her Goldilock curls.

"The evangelical world is in shock today after a bizarre incident destroyed the scandal-plagued Ministry of the Air. Luke Revere and an undisclosed number of followers committed mass suicide in an orgy of violence reminiscent of the Jim Jones cult."

File videotape of the Heaven on Earth retreat showed a smiling Revere surrounded by hundreds of beaming followers. "The bloodbath occurred at his Duchess County bible camp." The file footage vanished. Scenes of the massacre came on-screen. Atwood was silent as every corpse-strewn area was shown. Bodies littered the church and the village green.

Atwood's face returned. "Actual footage of the massacre was made available to *Action News.* It seems Luke Revere had just addressed a sermon to his Ministry of the Air fellowship. It was videotaped. So were the events that followed."

An enraged Luke Revere sprayed death into the deacons in front of the stage.

"Apparently a group in Revere's inner organization tried to stop the mass slaughter. An unidentified motorcyclist fired warning shots while others herded them into a bus. The driver of the bus returned for more passengers, but wasn't seen again. He is believed dead along with the others who tried to prevent Revere's genocidal directive."

Karen Atwood reviewed the connections to porn star Melonie Grand, the porn murders, and Peggy Revere's death. She ended her newscast with a late-breaking report that several more groups of Revere's followers committed mass suicide in pockets throughout the city. "An incredible array of deadly automatic weapons were found at each location shortly after the self-inflicted massacres."

She looked off-camera while another sheet of news copy was handed to her.

"Unimpeachable sources have provided *Action News* with information linking Revere's organization to several well-known political and financial figures across the country. A forthcoming exposé promises to topple corrupt electronic evangelists and a number of senators, congressmen, and their aides."

She smiled. "*Action News* will keep you up to date on further developments in this tragedy. Until then, this is Karen Atwood saying, 'Have a nice tomorrow'."

Peter Cruz threw an impromptu cast party on the last day of filming for *Starlet*. The porn director had wrapped up the shooting in less than a week after he was given the all-clear signal. That, plus the fact that they were all alive, was reason enough to celebrate in the hotel suite that appeared in the last scene of the film.

Mick Porter was glad that it was over. These weren't his kind of people, except possibly for Barbara, the special-effects girl. But even she had her kinks.

Almost as if she were reading his mind, Barbara zeroed in on him. She was wearing a low-cut black sun-dress and a floppy hat. Heart-shaped sunglasses vamped up the stunning outfit.

"The dragon lady approaches," Mick said.

"Now's as good a time as any for an approach," she shot back. "Were you going to leave without saying good-bye?" She clinked the ice in her mixed drink. Barbara sipped, then stepped in close to fix his tie that didn't need fixing.

Mick looked down at her pretty face and beyond. "How could I leave without one last look?"

"Mmmmn. In that case." She reached into her tiny black handbag and handed him a clipping of two movies playing at the Midtown Classic Cinema. *Bourbon Street Shadows* and *Kiss and Kill* were the features. A Shadow flick and a Fu Manchu. "You want to go?" she said.

She'd done her homework, Mick thought. He remembered their past conversation about his kind of movies. "You asking me for a date?"

The redhead bit her lip. "Yeah," she said. "I'm asking."

"Can't do it," he said.

"I *thought* so," she huffed.

"I prefer to do the asking."

"Oh."

"Would you like to take in a couple of flicks?" Mick asked.

Barbara grinned.

Across the room, Melonie Grand was in her glory. She had a clinging gown, a diamond necklace traveling down her spectacular chest, and gorgeous blond hair spun from gold. Her voice was breathless, her eyes were hungry. She had separated herself from the party to speak to Dartanian. In a way, she was almost sad that her body no longer needed looking after. It was the last day of security, the last hour in fact. She'd made one last play for him and missed.

"What are your plans?" she asked.

"Business as usual," he said. "And you?" he asked.

She glanced at the phone. For the past hour she'd been expecting a call from Hollywood. But then, a lot of actresses were expecting calls from Hollywood. Melonie had it in her head that the instant she finished *Starlet* the movie moguls would beat down her door.

"I'm not sure, actually," Melonie said. "There are some porn offers, but I'm planning to go straight."

Dartanian smiled and raised his glass. "A toast," he said. "For when you get there."

Reverend Soames stepped into the tenth-floor office. His coal black face was tight with anger. "*Mister* Dartanian," he said.

"Yes?"

"A package of money arrived at my church this morning. More money than I have ever seen. There's a note on Revere's stationery saying the half-million dollars was earmarked for my congregation. It was signed Luke Revere. But I don't think it's a real signature."

"You don't," Dartanian said.

"Right. I think it's a fake. And I think it's blood money!"

"Why tell me?"

"Let's put it together," Soames said. "Your man comes round, you come round, asking questions about Revere. All of a sudden Revere's a gone man. That makes me part of murder, baby."

"Revere took many lives in the past," Dartanian said. "He would've killed hundreds more with his lunatic hit squads. I think it's fortunate he committed suicide when he did."

"Don't toy with me," Soames warned.

"Nothing I say will convince you of my innocence. But Revere's people fleeced that money from gullible souls. Now it's in good hands. Use it in good conscience."

"It *will* be used," Soames said. "My people need it. But I want you to know I don't buy this suicide fantasy you whipped up for the media."

Dartanian gazed calmly at the preacher, projecting the picture of innocence. "Television does have a way of distorting things. Take Revere for example. He wrecked the spiritual life of millions of Americans." He paused. "Revere's gone now. Thank God."

"Not this time," Soames said. "I want you to know that *I* know what went down." He spun around and stormed to the door. He turned and said, "You are one damned soul, Mr. Dartanian."

Dartanian watched him go. "You're probably right," he said. *But there's no other way.*